Lady Barbara's Dilemma

by

Marjorie Farrell

DI026826

Ⓢ A SIGNET BOOK

SIGNET
Published by the Penguin Group
Penguin Books USA Inc., 375 Hudson Street,
New York, New York 10014, U.S.A.
Penguin Books Ltd, 27 Wrights Lane,
London W8 5TZ, England
Penguin Books Australia Ltd, Ringwood,
Victoria, Australia
Penguin Books Canada Ltd, 10 Alcorn Avenue,
Toronto, Ontario, Canada M4V 3B2
Penguin Books (N.Z.) Ltd, 182-190 Wairau Road,
Auckland 10, New Zealand

Penguin Books Ltd, Registered Offices:
Harmondsworth, Middlesex, England

First published by Signet,
an imprint of New American Library,
a division of Penguin Books USA Inc.

First Printing, March, 1993
10 9 8 7 6 5 4 3 2 1

To my good friends, old and new,
who have given me the support
a writer needs, especially Ann and
Fran Grady, Cathy Schwartz,
Bob Schwartz, Nancy Nimmich,
Joan Dolamore, Barbara Vacarr,
and Mary Jo Putney.

ACKNOWLEDGMENTS

This book would have been impossible to write without Todd Endelman's *The Jews of Georgian England: 1714–1830*. Any errors are mine.

And my thanks to Aly Bain, Alasdair Fraser, Brian McNeill, Daniel Stepner, John Gibbons, and Voice of the Turtle—musicians extraordinaire—for hours of enjoyment and inspiration.

Prologue

"Lord Alexander has arrived, my lord. Shall I send him in?"

"Yes, Larkin." The Duke of Strathyre, who had, to all appearances, been engrossed in a political memoir, put down his book and moved from his comfortable sofa to sit behind his desk. It was a strategic move. The duke, who was a consummate politician, never did anything casually. He was a small man, his grandson was a tall one: therefore he would sit on a harder, higher chair while his grandson sank into the furniture. Not that the duke was conscious of his strategy. He might be small and slender and white-haired, but he was also one of the most powerful men in either Scotland or England, and his techniques for maintaining that power had become habit.

By the time Alec MacLeod entered the library, the duke was seemingly engrossed in the latest estate reports, and his grandson had to clear his throat several times before the old man even looked up.

"Ah, Alec. How delightful to see you. Sit down, lad, sit down."

Alec, who stood almost a foot taller than his grandfather, smiled to himself at the "lad." He might not be a politician, but he was familiar with the duke's tactics, having seen his father outmaneuvered time after time. He sank into the sofa, and semi-seriously sent up a silent prayer that he would succeed in keeping his resolve straight, even if he couldn't keep his back so.

After a few moments, it was clear that he was going to have to be the first one to break the silence. He hated to give even a little ground to his grandsire, but better the sacrifice of a little ground now than the whole field later.

"You wished to speak with me, Grandfather?"

"Ah, yes," said the duke, tearing himself away from the papers in front of him. "Yes."

"Well, here I am, then."

"Yes, here you are," said the duke, looking over this young man who was so close to him in blood, but so different in appearance from both his father and grandfather.

The duke and his son were both black-haired and brown-eyed. Small of stature and slender of build, they projected an elegant strength. Alec resembled his mother's side of the family, being auburn-haired, blue-eyed, and tall. If the duke and the marquess were to be compared with weapons, they would most resemble rapiers. Alec, on the other hand, was like a claymore, the heavy broadsword wielded by his ancestors.

Except for his hands. His fingers were long and slender, surprisingly so for such a big man, and were the one feature he and his grandfather had in common, in appearance at least. Not, however, in how they used them.

Right now the duke's hands were still, placed on the desk in front of him. They were remarkably young-looking hands for a man of sixty-eight, well-manicured, white, and smooth. They were also powerful hands, hands that had beckoned and dismissed and signed away properties and lives for years.

Alec's hands were rarely still. When he spoke, they were as expressive as his tongue. His hands were more likely to ruffle a child's hair or clap a friend on the shoulder than to gesture commands. And, above all, they were a musician's hands.

"Your father informs me that you have still not chosen a career, Alec."

"You know that is not true, Grandfather. I have known for a long time what I wish to do."

"So it is the law, the government, or the church?" queried the duke, in a most annoyingly feigned ignorance.

"You know it is not any of those, Grandfather. I am a violinist and wish to make music my life. Nay, it already is my life," replied his grandson.

"The grandson of the Duke of Strathyre and the son of the Marquess of Doune cannot make his living playing the fiddle," said the duke contemptuously.

"On the contrary, Grandfather," said Alec with a touch of amusement in his voice, "it is the only sphere in which I have enough talent to make my living. I have no head for the intricacies of our judicial system, not enough hypocrisy for government service, and too little piety for the church."

"You know very well what I mean," answered the duke, his grandson's insouciance almost making him lose control. "No grandson of mine will end up a professional musician. It is one thing to play for family and friends' private entertainment. It is quite another to traipse across the concert stages of England and the Continent."

"What I wish to do, as you well know, is to continue my studies in London and eventually to give most of my energy to composition. Although I will not deny that I may perform outside of social occasions once in a while."

"And how will you support yourself, do you suppose? I can't imagine that the odd violin sonata will keep food on the table, much less support you in the style which befits your station."

The duke had not raised his voice, nor did he sound as if he was discussing anything of great importance. But Alec, who had vowed he would not lose his temper, could not keep his voice free of emotion. When he felt something, his voice vibrated with it, be it anger or desire. While women usually responded to his expressiveness, he knew that he was at a disadvantage with the duke. His fire might melt an icy woman, but not his grandsire. He took a deep breath to calm himself before he spoke again.

"I had intended, of course, to live on my inheritance from Grandmother."

"Your father and I have agreed that it would not have been your grandmother's intention that you use her legacy to pursue such a foolish course. As her executor, I intend to stop your allowance unless you agree to pursue a career more appropriate to your position."

Alec willed himself to remain in his seat. He knew that if he attempted to change the balance of power, even physically, he was lost. His grandfather had wanted him to feel at a disadvantage sucked down by the sofa. Well, let him still believe that he was.

"You know, my lord, that Grandmother supported me in my music."

"When you were younger, oh, yes," replied the duke, with a dismissive wave of his hand. "But I assure you, she did not intend for you to fiddle away your inheritance."

"And I have no intention of doing so. The income would be quite adequate for my needs."

"And what of those of wife and children?"

"I have no interest in marriage at the moment. And there is no reason for me to think about it yet. After all, you and my father and brother are in excellent health, and likely to lead long and happy lives. I only wish to be allowed to do the same."

"How do you *know* that a life centered around music will make you happy?"

"How did you know that politics was your forte, Grandfather?" Alec countered. "One knows."

"What you do not know is how it would be to live without the money and privilege you have been used to. It is one thing to fiddle Scottish dances with Gower, and quite another to make a name in London."

"If I can play a strathspey by Matthew Gower to his satisfaction, I am sure that my performance of Mozart should be expert enough for an orchestra," replied Alec, the smile on his face concealing his rising anger. Gower had enjoyed his grandfather's patronage for years and had been Alec's teacher for much of that time. Gower's original compositions and his versions of traditional tunes were familiar all over Scotland. And though a *ton* audience appreciated a sonata over a reel and a violinist over a fiddler, thought Alec, he knew that a dance tune called for as much virtuosity as a classical piece.

"Be that as it may," said the duke, examining his perfectly manicured nails, "your grandmother's money is in my hands and I will not continue your allowance if you refuse to give up your music." The duke sat there, confident that, as usual, he had bested his opponent. With no money to live on, his grandson would have to see reason. And after he became a solicitor (for surely that would be the most appropriate career for him), he could play music for his own and his family's enjoyment. No need to give it up entirely. It was not, after all, that he did not secretly appreciate his grandson's talent. It was just that he wanted it kept in its proper place.

Alec, however, knew that his grandfather had lost. Because power and privilege and money were all important to the duke, he could not imagine living without them. Nor could he understand what music was to Alec: something he could not live without. Perhaps it was because he was relatively removed from the possibility of inheritance, perhaps it was because he had inherited his mother's mercurial temperament rather than his father's staidness; whatever it was, Alec could live without money if he had to. What he had hoped, however, was that he could manage to have both.

"You are convinced that I could never succeed on my own as a musician, Grandfather? That denying me Grandmother's bequest will convince me of that?"

"Oh, you have talent, my boy. But whoever heard of a duke's grandson living on nothing and liking it?"

"I have a bargain to strike with you, then."

"Yes?"

"Let me have one year as a musician. If I cannot survive on my talent alone, or if I hate it, then I will agree to enter whatever profession you feel is most appropriate for me." Alec tried to strike a balance in tone between bravado and hesitancy. He wanted his grandfather to believe that he was not quite sure of his dedication and his resilience.

"Are you offering me a wager, Alec?" asked the duke, his studied indifference finally cracking.

"I suppose you could call it that," replied his grandson. And one that I can't lose, thought Alec. For I intend to live by my music anyway, if that becomes necessary.

"And what if you do survive through the year? Then what?" queried the duke.

"If I can make my own way for a year, then you will re-instate my allowance and let me go my own way."

His grandfather's eyes gleamed. While he was no inveterate gambler, he enjoyed a game of chance as well as anyone. Alec would come home defeated in six months or less; of that he was certain. And maybe it was a good idea to let him get this obsession with music out of his system. If he tried and, as was inevitable, failed, then he would enter the law with much more enthusiasm than if he had been forced to it.

"I will agree, upon one condition," said the duke.

"And that?"

"That for one year from today you live incognito. No one is to know you are my grandson. That way we both will know that no one hired you only because of your family name. And that you spend the year in England."

Alec had envisioned himself in the south, and was confident enough of his skill that he had never intended to trade on the family connections.

"Agreed, Grandfather," he said, rising from the sofa at last and approaching the desk. "Here is my hand on it."

The duke looked up into his grandson's blue eyes, and seeing the gleam of satisfaction there, had the fleeting sensation that he had been outmaneuvered. Since no one had ever succeeded in besting him, however, he dismissed the idea immediately and rose to shake his grandson's hand. And so the two men parted, each confident that the end of the year would see him the winner.

1

"Simon."

"Hunnhh."

"Simon."

The Duke of Sutton rolled over toward his wife and pulled her close to him, fitting her backside against him and running his hands across her rounding belly. "And how is the heir to the dukedom this morning?"

Judith sighed in satisfaction as she felt her husband's hands caress her, and had a hard time pushing his fingers away as they moved lower. It was early morning and there was nothing she liked better than making love and then going back to sleep for a few hours. And as she had noticed with her first pregnancy, her pleasure in lovemaking increased when she was carrying a child. Six months into her term she had felt idyllic with Sophy and did so again with the "heir," as they laughingly called the small resident of her body. She was well past morning sickness, felt a remarkable sense of well-being, and was proudly rounded rather than clumsily elephantine, as one became in the last weeks of pregnancy.

"Very well, Simon. But I did not wake you to make love, but to talk," she said as she turned to face him. "I was thinking about Barbara."

Simon groaned in mock despair. "Thinking about your latest coze with Barbara while your husband goes mad with unsatisfied desire!"

"Mad with desire indeed. You were barely awake a few

minutes ago. No, now be serious, Simon," Judith protested, as her husband traced his fingers over her face and down to her mouth and ran his thumb over her lips.

"Oh, I assure you, I am quite serious," he said fervently, as he leaned forward to kiss her. Judith's mouth opened to speak again, and then, feeling his probing tongue, she gave up for the moment the idea of an early-morning discussion.

A half an hour later, just as Simon was drifting off, Judith spoke again.

"Simon."

"Not again, your grace?"

"No. This time I want you to listen. I am worried about Barbara."

"Unnhh."

"Simon, wake up!" This time the Duchess of Sutton poked the duke unceremoniously in the ribs and finally succeeded in getting his undivided, unamorous attention. He rolled over on his back, pulled another pillow under his head, and folding his arms over his chest, said with exaggerated patience, "I'm listening, Judith."

"And about time."

"Now, what is worrying you about Barbara?"

"I don't know exactly," confessed his wife. "That is," she continued, as Simon groaned again, "I know that she is not herself, that she is unhappy, but she does not talk about it. In fact, she hardly talks to me anymore except about the least important matters. And she told me the other day that she is going to discontinue her studies with Signor Cavalcanti."

"She may only feel that she needs a break from her practice. After all, she has been working with him for four years."

"But that is precisely it, Simon. Barbara has been devoted to her music for as long as I can remember."

"Do you think she is in love?"

"I don't think so. Although that itself may be the problem," added Judith thoughtfully.

"She spent quite a bit of time with Peter Rushcliffe during the Little Season, didn't she?"

"Yes. I am sure that he was developing a *tendre* for her. Whether she did for him, I don't know. But she certainly gave him more attention than she has anyone for years. If he chooses to come up for this Season, I am sure he has a good chance of winning her. I only want her to be as happy as we are, Simon."

"We are, aren't we, Judith?" said the duke, gently stroking his wife's hair.

"Frighteningly so."

"Nothing to be frightened of, my love," replied her husband, pulling her closer and burying his face in her neck.

2

Lady Barbara Stanley absently fingered the keys of the fortepiano. She had been in the music room for the better part of an hour and still had not been able to put her mind to her practice.

Two weeks ago she had turned twenty-six. Each Season since her first had gotten less and less enjoyable. Early on she had seen her contemporaries married off, and now there was a new generation of young women. Not precisely a new generation, she reminded herself humorously, but it felt that way. Seasons had come and gone, suitors had filled her dance cards, sent her flowers, and a few had gone even so far as to make her offers. She had been attracted by none of them.

The trouble is, she thought, I have been holding Simon and Judith's marriage before me as a model of what I want. And that is foolish, for their marriage is a rare thing in our circle. The young ladies that come and go are not holding out for a love match.

At the thought of Simon and Judith, her fingers became still. The fact that her closest friend was so happy should make her happy. And it had, for a year or two. She had felt a part of the magic, and when Sophy was born, become her beloved godmother. But Judith's interests were different now, centered around her family and her new pregnancy. It was not that the Suttons were not inclusive: they had always made Barbara feel like a member of the family. But Judith was less interested in discussions about art and literature and more in conversations about when a child should begin to learn her letters and how one felt in the early months of pregnancy. In fact, she had become quite friendly with the new Countess of Alverstoke, who was expecting her first child the month after Judith her second.

Barbara liked Miranda; who could not? But she was young, completely wrapped up in her husband and expected child, and found Judith to be a great support, just as she had been in the weeks before Miranda's marriage. Whenever Barbara called on Judith these days, it seemed that the countess was there before her, playing with Sophy or engaging in conversations with Judith about the details of labor and delivery. Or talking about the paradoxical reactions of doting husbands when faced with the reality of a first child.

Barbara would drink her tea and eat her cake during these conversations and feel like a spinster of advanced age. It was not that Judith was willfully ignoring her. It was just that her family concerns were so absorbing. As well they should be, thought Barbara. I have no right to feel resentful.

But she couldn't help it. She did feel both resentful and jealous . . . and even angry. In fact, sometimes when she walked into the house on Brook Street, she almost hated Judith and Simon for their happiness, and it was all she could do to utter polite comments and keep a spiteful tone out of her voice.

Where once she had shared all her deepest feelings with Judith, now she was afraid to talk to her at all for fear she would reveal her ugly anger and jealousy. How could one say to one's best friend: "I resent your happiness," when that friend was always trying to share her happiness? How could one say: "I feel excluded," when Simon and Judith were always encouraging her to join them? Above all, how could one say, like a small child: "I thought *I* was your best friend, but now you spend your time with Lady Alverstoke"? And so Barbara said less and less and was careful to visit when there was likely to be company so the gradual loss of their intimate talks was less noticeable.

For a while, before her emotions had reached their present state, her music had been her refuge. The past four years she had concentrated on her studies with Signor Cavalcanti and made remarkable progress. Barbara knew she was now the equal of any professional performer. But what was the point of knowing one was good enough for the concert stage when one could never walk onto one? And so, for the past few months, practice felt meaningless, until she finally decided to give it up. "Oh, only for a few months," she had assured her teacher and her brother and her friends. "I need a short rest, after all these years."

She had thought she would miss it, but she didn't. She had wandered into the music room this morning to see if she could rekindle her interest, but here she was, as blue-deviled as ever, and music was not going to lift her mood.

The only times her mood lightened at all these days was when she thought about the coming Season. She had noticed Peter Rushcliffe's growing interest in her this past autumn, and of all the men who had come her way over the years, he interested her the most. When they waltzed, she had felt pleasure in their closeness, and enjoyed their conversations. She was determined to look upon this Season as a decisive one. If she was very lucky, she would find a potential for passion with the Marquess of Wardour. At the very least, she would discover whether their feelings for one another could support a marriage. She thought they could, hoped they could, for if he made an offer she was determined to accept. It would be delightful if she could love him, but she knew she could respect him and was ready to settle for respect and affection. She was tired of being "Auntie Barbara" to Sophy and to Robin's two boys. It was time she had a husband and children of her own.

3

The Season started slowly, with Lady Harlech's ball the third week of April expected to be the first real crush. The Duke and Duchess of Sutton planned to attend, for Lord Harlech was a noted Whig. It was likely to be one of Judith's few large events this year because of her pregnancy, and for that reason she was determined to make the most of the occasion and host a small dinner party of friends beforehand.

"Robin and Diana. Jeremy and Miranda. Nora and Sam. Barbara . . . whom shall I invite for Barbara, Simon?" asked Judith as she wrote out her invitations.

"Wardour?"

"No, no."

"I thought you said he appeared interested?"

"Yes, he did, but it would be much too soon and too obvious," Judith explained. "Can you think of anyone?"

"What about David Treves?" Simon suggested after a few moments' thought.

"Yes, he would be perfect. Someone who shares an interest in music. A potential friend but not suitor."

The evening of her dinner party all of the guests but one had arrived when Judith came down a little late and a little breathless. "Sophy always seems to demand one more story when she knows that guests are coming," she explained. Diana gave her an indulgent smile. Judith had always been unconventional in her parenting habits, but Simon seemed not to disapprove. She herself, however, much as she loved her twins, was always grateful to turn them over to their nurse, and Robin, thank goodness, encouraged her to do so.

Judith sat herself down next to Viscount Vane and joined in the debate over Ireland. In a few minutes all, with the exception of Diana, Barbara, and Nora, who were discussing Miss Austen's final novel, were caught up in the debate, and the butler had to announce the final guest twice.

"Sir David Treves, your grace."

Barbara looked up first, for Judith had told her that Sir David would be her partner at dinner. Her friend had said it straightforwardly and with none of the assumed nonchalance of one who was making an attempt at matchmaking, so Barbara had decided Sir David would be older and not attractive. In reality, he looked only a few years older than she, and was very handsome, albeit in an un-English way. She wondered idly if he was Welsh on his mother's side, for he had the black hair, brown eyes, and dark skin that occur amongst Celtic people. Or perhaps Spanish, she thought, as she noticed the clean, sharp planes of his face and aquiline nose.

Simon, who had finally heard the second announcement, stood up and made his way to the door. Sir David tactfully moved forward to meet him, Barbara noticed with approval, and extended his hand and greeted the duke so Simon would know immediately where he was.

"Come," said Simon, "let me introduce you to a few of the ladies before I pull you into our debate."

Although she had seen it again and again, Barbara always marveled at how easily, despite his blindness, Simon moved when he was in a familiar place. He knew the exact placement of the furniture and immediately located Barbara and her companions by the sounds of their voices.

"David, I would like you to meet Lady Barbara Stanley, Lady Vane, and Lady Stanley."

David bowed.

"Lady Stanley and Lady Barbara are sisters-in-law," Simon explained.

"I have heard you are a talented musician, Lady Barbara," said Treves with more than polite interest.

"You have heard correctly," interjected Simon. "I'll leave you two to discuss your passion."

"Do you play an instrument, Sir David?" queried Lady Vane.

"Unfortunately not. My father pulled me into the family business years ago, and so I am only an educated listener. But a passionate one, and I have had the opportunity, from time to time, of helping a musician on his way."

"And your family's business is . . . ?" asked Diana in a tone that bordered on the impolite. Barbara looked at her sideways, puzzled by her sudden coolness and suspecting that she knew perfectly well what the Treves family business was.

"Mr. Joshua Treves is the head of Treves and Sons, which contributed so much to Wellington's campaign," said Lady Vane. "I am delighted to see you again, David."

"And I you, Nora. I mean, my lady."

"No, we had agreed on first names, David."

"Thank you, Nora."

"We were just discussing Miss Austen's *Persuasion*. But perhaps you would prefer a more animated discussion," said Nora, nodding her head in the direction of Simon and the others.

"I think I will stay here if I may? It is not every day that a man can be surrounded by both beauty and intelligence."

The compliment was commonplace, and although Barbara heard it as sincere, she also had the feeling that some sort of challenge was being offered. Diana clearly disapproved of something in Treves' background and had expressed it in the most convoluted and English of ways. Treves could have taken the easy way out and joined the others. Barbara was glad that he hadn't. She loved her sister-in-law, but like Judith, couldn't help noticing that the Diana who had been a bit wild as a young woman had turned into the most sedate wife with the most conventional of ideas.

Sir David was obviously someone who liked literature as well as music, thought Barbara as she listened to his conversation with Nora. Diana and Barbara had remained silent, Diana to show her disapproval and Barbara to see if she could learn something about her dinner partner. She wondered if Sir David was a less-than-subtle attempt at matchmaking on Judith's part when he led her into dinner.

"Have you been acquainted with the duke and duchess for a long time, Lady Barbara?" asked Treves after they had been seated.

"I have known Simon all my life, and Judith since my school days," she replied. "In fact, I feel partly responsible for their marriage." When Treves looked at her questioningly, she said, "But that is a long story and I'm afraid it would bore you. Have you known Simon very long?"

"I met him briefly before Waterloo, and renewed my acquaintance over this past year."

"Can I assume, then, that you are interested in the same political questions?"

"Yes, we have the same broad principles, and I have a particular interest of my own," replied Sir David slowly.

"Have you ever thought of standing for a seat in the House yourself, Sir David?"

"I have thought of it often, Lady Barbara, but there are certain difficulties . . ." Treves lèt his voice trail off and Barbara was unwilling to pry further. Perhaps his family preferred him to stay with the business.

"Tell me something about your music, Lady Barbara."

"There is not much to tell," replied Barbara, conscious that for some reason she wanted to tell Sir David everything about her discouragement. There was an air of sympathy about him and she had heard something in his voice just now that made her think that he too knew something about frustrated dreams.

"Somehow I find that hard to believe," said Treves.

"You are right. There is a lot to tell. Too much," Barbara said, her voice trembling slightly.

"Well, we do have a few more courses before the confections," said Treves with an encouraging smile.

"I will put it in a nutshell so as not to bore you," said Barbara. "I have been studying for many years, I have some talent, and because I am a woman I will never be able to exercise that talent in the way I wish. And so I have given up my lessons. There. I have said it. And to a complete stranger! But there is something about you, Sir David, that encourages confidence. And when you spoke of certain difficulties earlier, I had the idea that perhaps you too have wanted something you can't have?"

"I believe that we do have that in common, Lady Barbara. You, by virtue of being a woman and a lady, will never appear on a concert stage, and I, by virtue of being born a Jew, will never sit in Parliament or even enter a profession."

"But your name is Treves," said Barbara, without thinking.

"You are pronouncing it the English way. Originally it was Spanish."

"Yes, I thought you looked Spanish or Portuguese. But you are every inch the English gentleman," protested Barbara.

"My people have been quite successful in adopting the culture of their host country," he said with a touch of irony. "It is the way we have survived. And I *am* an English gentleman. The Treveses have been here since Cromwell readmitted the Jews."

"Then you are one of the Sephardim?" said Barbara, pronouncing the word carefully.

"Correct. I am surprised that you did not know immediately when you heard my father's name. Lady Diana recognized it. . . ."

"So that is why she was rude!" exclaimed Barbara.

"Oh, I wouldn't say rude. Just subtly disapproving of my

presence. I may be every inch the English gentleman, but there are homes in which I would not be welcome."

"I feel very ignorant," confessed Barbara. "Of course, I was aware that much of Wellington's financial support came from . . ." She hesitated.

"Jews. It is all right, my lady, you can say it. The word itself is not an insult," said Treves sardonically.

"What I meant was that I didn't recognize your father's name. I have heard of Moses Montefiore, of course. Simon and Sam have spoken of him often. They have also spoken of Jewish emancipation. Is that the particular issue to which you referred?"

"Indeed it is, Lady Barbara, although I feel very alone in my concern. Most Jews seem satisfied with the degree of acceptance we have achieved. I am not. I wish full citizenship. The opportunity to send my son to a university. The right to vote. The right to live as the loyal English citizens that we already are. But it is hard to convince the English that we are English too."

"Well, we do have something in common," Barbara said. "We are both kept from full citizenship. Judith and I were quite fond of Mary Wollstonecraft when we were at school. I haven't thought of her in a while. Perhaps I need to reread her book and get back some of my youthful fervor for radical ideas. I must confess I have felt quite old lately."

"It would be ungentlemanly of me to even hazard a guess, but surely not old!"

"I am quite on the shelf."

"Nonsense."

"Not nonsense at all, Sir David. Judith is forever trying to match me up with someone. In fact, I was afraid you were another of her attempts," Barbara confessed with a becoming blush.

"I doubt it. Even the Duke and Duchess of Sutton are not so liberal as to consider a Jewish suitor for Lady Barbara Stanley."

"If I thought I could feel for you what Simon and Judith

feel for each other, I assure you your Jewishness would not matter, Sir David."

"Quite charmingly said, Lady Barbara. I think I thank you, although it was a rather backhanded compliment," replied David with a teasing smile.

"But you do not believe me?"

"No. However, that is not because I doubt your sincerity, but because of the ways of the world. But I am glad to hear that you have not fallen in love at first sight!"

Barbara blushed again. "Oh, dear, that didn't come out quite the way I meant it. But I can say I instantly *liked* you."

Treves laughed. "And I you. Perhaps we can be good friends, then? I would be most honored to accompany you to an occasional musicale and hope that someday I will have the privilege of hearing you play."

"Friends it is, then," agreed Barbara.

She felt better than she had in weeks. Her conversation with Sir David had reminded her of her talks with Judith. There had been instant rapport and openness. And with Judith so preoccupied, she could only rejoice that she had found a new friend.

4

Peter Rushcliffe, the Marquess of Wardour, was not present at the Harlech ball. He had only arrived in London late that afternoon, having traveled all day from Kent. He had hoped to be in town before the beginning of the new Season in order to have every possible opportunity of seeing Lady Barbara Stanley, but the week before he was to leave, his estate manager had presented him with three separate crises. The marquess was nothing if not a conscientious landowner and so he ignored his mother's suggestion that he leave it all to Evans.

In fact, had it not been for his planned courtship, he would not be going to London at all. He only went up for the Season infrequently, and had been there last autumn because his niece was getting married. Attending the festivities leading up to the wedding had led to more socializing than was usual for him, and that was how he had been introduced to Lady Barbara.

He had never experienced more than a passing attraction to a woman before Barbara Stanley. She was mature, a fact that pleased him. She was also a most attractive lady: tall enough so that he did not feel he towered over her, but not so tall that he didn't top her by a few inches. Hers was a classic English beauty, with her blond hair and blue eyes. He decided that the old adage that opposites attract was clearly wrong, for here, obviously, liked called to like. He himself was more serious than many of his contemporaries, he himself was above average height, and his hair was even a shade lighter than hers.

From the beginning he knew she would make him an excellent wife, and by the end of the Little Season, having received some encouragement from her, had decided, if all continued as it had begun, to make her an offer by the end of the spring.

He had, of course, no doubt that should he decide to make an offer, it would be accepted, for he was used to getting what he wanted. He had inherited the title when he was only ten, and had been supported, protected, and even a little spoiled by his mother and older sister. It was not that he got away with any wrongdoing. In fact, he had never been inclined, even as a child, to get into mischief. He had been a perfectly behaved boy and had grown up into a perfectly behaved young man. He never made unreasonable demands—or any demands. It was just that his mother and his sister had been so sympathetic to him being fatherless at such an early age that his every want was satisfied almost before it was expressed. Luckily he was not a greedy or a selfish young man, or he might have turned into a monster of egocentricity. Instead, he was a devoted son, caring brother, responsible landowner, and good neighbor. However, he always expected that things would go his way, for they always had. His was a subtle kind of pride, the kind that takes respect and privilege for granted, for the Wardours of Arundel were an old family, the title was an early one, and the property extensive.

The second day he was in Town, therefore, Wardour sent Barbara a small bouquet with a note informing her that he hoped to see her at the Whiting rout.

"Barbara, you look absolutely stunning."

"Thank you, Robin."

"I imagine that the dress will complement Wardour's coloring," added Robin with a wicked grin. "Do you expect him to be at the Whitings' tonight?"

Barbara blushed.

"Ah, a direct hit, I see," said her brother.

"Now, Robin, don't tease," chided Diana. "We are all aware that Wardour seemed attracted to Barbara in the fall. But let us wait and see what the Season brings."

"Thank you, Diana," said Barbara with a grateful smile. "I am happy to know that one member of my family respects my privacy," she continued with mock anger.

Robin looked not one whit remorseful. Brother and sister shared the same sense of humor and he knew Barbara was not really offended. But her blush had confirmed what he suspected: an interest in Wardour that went beyond anything she had felt for years. Her blush also diminished the mild sense of anxiety he had felt over the past week. Barbara had attended an opera and a concert in the company of the Vanes and Sir David Treves. Robin liked and respected Treves. But he was surprised to discover that despite his politics, he would not be happy seeing his sister marry a Jew.

"Of course, the Nile green that you wore to the opera only made Treves look handsomer." Robin couldn't resist any opportunity to tease, but this time he hoped his worries would be laid to rest.

"David and I are nothing but good friends, Robin. We discovered our mutual love of music at Simon and Judith's the other night, and it has been delightful to have his company, rather than my brother's, who has been known to fall asleep! Come, it is getting late," said Barbara, starting for the door.

Robin and Diana shared a look of relief and followed her to the carriage.

Lady Whiting always invited more people than her house could comfortably hold, and so it took the Stanleys a few minutes to go through the receiving line and search out Viscount Vane and Lord Alverstoke.

Barbara found herself aware of everyone, and listening

for the distinct tone of Wardour's voice. She was surprised at herself, pleasantly surprised, for surely this indicated that she was ready and willing to fall in love with him.

When they at last reached their friends, Barbara was delighted to see that one of their company was Wardour. He seemed equally delighted to see her. In fact, he had approached the viscount and immediately renewed their acquaintance precisely because he was the Stanleys' friend. He did not intend a subtle and slow courtship. He intended to win Barbara, and he intended to do it straightforwardly.

He was disappointed, therefore, when she could not offer him her first dance. But his disappointment was short-lived, for she offered him her first waltz. She had saved it on purpose, hoping that he would ask her.

Wardour waited patiently, and when they at last moved off onto the dance floor, neither was disappointed. The marquess was one of those rare dance partners whom one followed without being aware of following. The waltz was effortless, and they could not keep from smiling at each other in sheer enjoyment. She was pleasantly conscious that the steady pressure of his hand on her back did indeed raise her temperature more than could be expected from the exercise. And at one point in the dance, their fingers linked together naturally and unconsciously. When Wardour finally noticed, he gave her hand a squeeze before flattening her palm and holding her less intimately.

When the dance was over and he left to dance with his sister, Barbara realized that her legs were shaky and her cheeks flushed. It was such a relief to know that this Season might very well bring her everything she wished for that she felt a bit giddy, and moved next to Robin and placed her hand on his arm. When he asked if she were all right, she answered that she was just a little dizzy from her waltz. They smiled at each other in the same instant, both happy at the way things appeared to be working out.

And while Wardour was careful not to monopolize Barbara's attention, it was clear by the end of the evening that Lady Barbara Stanley had a serious suitor, and one, moreover, that she seemed to be taking seriously.

5

It became even more evident over the next few weeks that Wardour was indeed serious, and Barbara found herself liking him as much as she had suspected she would, although there were more than a few political issues on which Barbara suspected they would differ. It was clear that Wardour was a Tory, but one, Barbara realized, with a genuine concern for his people that went generations deep. It was obvious that he had compassion for the working classes, and although his political solutions seemed illogical to her, she was more than happy to change the subject when a major disagreement loomed.

Whenever the marquess approached her for a dance, while her heart might not leap up, it gave a most decidedly satisfying flutter. Their waltzes lived up to the promise of the first one. Wardour's touch was delightful, whether on the dance floor or helping her up into his curricle, and she went to bed wondering what it would feel like when he finally kissed her. For she knew he would, and she knew if it wasn't in the next few days, she could most probably maneuver them onto a private balcony to speed things along.

In the meantime, she was also enjoying her developing friendship with David Treves. They had gotten into the habit of attending a musicale at least once a week, accompanied by one or another of their mutual acquaintances. And when Barbara discovered while she was out with her groom that David was fond of early-morning rides, she suggested meeting in the park one day a week. Usually after an invigorating gallop, they would walk their horses and talk nonstop about anything and everything, for they had become fast friends.

On one particular morning David, who had happened to attend the same rout the previous evening, teased Barbara about the gossip he had been hearing. "I have heard that the odds are in favor of a betrothal before the end of the Season between Lady Barbara Stanley and the Marquess of Wardour. Would I be premature in congratulating you?" he asked with a teasing grin.

"Much too premature. We haven't even kissed yet," she replied without thinking. Her hand flew up to her mouth in horror at what she had said.

David laughed out loud.

"Oh, David, you are too dangerous to be with," confessed Barbara. "I feel so comfortable with you that I don't think before I speak. I talk to you just as I used to talk to Judith. I suppose, having blurted that out, I must either pretend that I didn't or explain."

"Am I to understand from your previous statement, Lady Barbara," said David with mock solemnity, "that you honestly will admit the matter of kissing into your decision-making about an eligible suitor?"

"It isn't just my decision, you know."

"Oh, but the man will ask you, Barbara. The signs are all there. The question is rather what you will answer. And does your answer depend on how well he kisses?"

"I think I will answer him 'yes,' and yes, I think my answer will partly depend on how I feel when he kisses me. For I have already told you that Judith and Robin are my models in this. I've been spoiled in that the two people closest to me have found marriages where passion plays a prominent part."

"Yes, I have become quite envious myself, listening to you," said David, albeit with a trace of cynicism in his voice.

"And what of you, my friend. It is your turn to be embarrassed. Is there anyone in your life whom you have been kissing or wanting to kiss?"

"Now, Lady Barbara, you are aware, although it is not spoken of in polite company—but then we have agreed not to be polite—that most men have some woman in their lives whom they have been . . . ah . . . kissing."

"You will not put me to the blush again, David. Of course I know that. And of course you know what I was talking about. Is there anyone you care about? Have you thought of marriage yet?"

"Oh, I've thought of it. My grandfather and father will let me think of nothing else," he replied bitterly.

"This sounds like a sensitive topic. I am sorry I teased you about it, David. You need not continue," said Barbara with ready sympathy. "Close friends need to respect privacy as well as share intimacies, you know."

"No, I don't mind speaking of it with you. The question for me," he continued, "will never be one of passion. I am, as you once noted, every inch the English gentleman, and as such, I will choose my bride for practical reasons, not sentimental ones. And, of course, since I am also *not* the typical English gentleman, the process is a bit more complicated."

"Do you feel that you must marry a woman of your own faith?"

"What faith is that? You are a woman of my own faith, Barbara. A woman who is educated and intelligent and who appreciates music with all her heart and soul, as I do. Although you are an artist, as I am not."

"But you have a splendid voice, David," Barbara interjected.

"Thank you. But to continue, you are a person of some wealth and position in your community, as I am in mine. And a woman with interest in the important questions of our time. Being Jewish has nothing to do with all that. You know, we are quite lucky we are only good friends," said David, turning in his saddle to face her.

"Why is that?"

"Because were we romantically inclined we never could marry."

"But you told me your uncle married a Christian."

"Ah, yes, but a woman of lower rank than you, whose family was willing to sell her to the highest bidder, even though he was a Jew. I don't want to buy a wife."

"There must be girls from other Jewish families to whom you are introduced?"

"Yes. Our socializing works much like yours. But I haven't met anyone I can talk to, much less one who has kindled any feeling of attraction. But this is all too serious to worry about further on such a glorious morning, my dear friend. Come, let's have another gallop to clear our heads. And I hope that by next time we meet, we will have Wardour's kiss to talk about!"

6

It was more than a week before Barbara had anything to report, and she was beginning to wonder if Wardour was planning to make his offer without attempting any kisses at all. She sincerely hoped not, for although she was almost sure she would accept him, she still wanted to know that she would enjoy kissing Wardour as much as she enjoyed dancing with him. Unfortunately, every time she had tried to find a few moments alone with him, someone had spoiled her plans by joining them in conversation. And if it weren't someone joining their tête-à-tête, it was some pushing mama, introducing her daughter, and pulling Lady Barbara off for a coze. Some mothers never despair, even when a man has clearly indicated his interest, she would think as she was dragged off.

Finally, on the night of the Langtons' ball, when Barbara complained of being quite warm from their last waltz, Wardour solicitously asked if she wanted a breath of fresh air. Fortunately, all their friends seemed to be on the other side of the room, and they reached a window uninterrupted. And when they got there, Barbara, who was fully intending to pull Wardour out onto the balcony if she had to, was pleasantly surprised when he asked in a low voice if she would prefer moving outside. She nodded her head in assent and as they stepped out, Wardour pulled the French doors halfway closed behind him.

"Ah, there is a breeze here," Barbara said with a sigh.

She *had* been hot after the last dance, for the weather was sultry for the end of May. Wardour brought the back of his hand up to her cheek.

"You are quite warm, Lady Barbara. I hope our waltz was not too much for you?" He paused, and then continued, "And yet, I hope that we both feel some warmth that is not directly related to the weather or our exertion."

His hand was still against her cheek and Barbara reached up and, linking her fingers with his, moved both their hands to his cheek, a little surprised at her own boldness.

"We do seem to be suffering from the same condition," she said softly.

Wardour leaned down and kissed her lightly on the mouth. "I hope that our condition has a similar cause," he whispered. "I am warm from wanting to kiss you, but I fear," he said, "that if I kiss you again neither of us will cool off."

Barbara felt a thrill go through her as he lowered his head and she felt his breath against her neck. She closed her eyes and lifted her face and Wardour kissed her again, this time a little more insistently. His lips explored hers, but just as she began to respond and her mouth began to relax and open under his, he pulled back. Her eyes opened wide with surprise and disappointment.

"I must ask you something before I forget myself," Wardour said solemnly.

Barbara wanted to say, "Yes, yes, ask away and I'll answer and let us get back to what is truly important." In truth, for all her anticipation of the moment, she was so distracted that she didn't guess what he was about to ask.

"I should talk to your father first, I know, and I fully intended to," he continued. "But I fear I have lost control over my good intentions, and must ask now, for the sake of your reputation as well as my own peace of mind."

Lost control? wondered Barbara. Oh, let us lose control!

"Lady Barbara, I do not think I am mistaken that we have an affection for one another. And this evening proves that we respond to one another in . . . other ways. Will you do me the honor of consenting to be my wife?"

Now that the moment had come, Barbara felt herself go from hot to cold in an instant. *Did* she want to spend her life with this man? She thought so. She thought they could make each other comfortable and happy. And this evening had proved they would be physically compatible, if one could judge by a kiss or two. Did she love him as Judith loved Simon? She didn't know, but she did know she was tired of waiting. And she also knew she wanted another kiss.

"Yes, yes, I will," she replied quietly.

Wardour smiled. It was a spontaneous smile, which lit up his whole face, but it also had in it a trace of satisfaction. There was no surprise on his face, no lover's insecurity. He had, to judge by his smile, expected her answer to be yes. As why should he not, she told herself. But still, it bothered her a little.

Just then Wardour leaned down and kissed her again, and the moment of doubt passed. This third kiss was the best of all, for as her lips parted, he pulled her closer and pushed his tongue gently into her mouth. She wanted the kiss to go on for a long time, but he pulled away from her again, saying, "I wouldn't like us to be discovered like this, my dear, even though we are now betrothed. People would say that I only proposed to avoid a scandal. I will ride out to Ashurst tomorrow and talk to your father."

Barbara found herself reluctant to start thinking practically. She knew he was right. It would be embarrassing to be caught in his arms. And he did have to speak to her father before an announcement could be made, so she swallowed her disappointment that they couldn't go on exploring the delights of kissing for another hour or so and smoothed her hair and smiled up at him.

"You are right, Peter. Although I hate to go back, I suppose we must."

He dropped a quick kiss on her head. "Soon we will be able to kiss as long as we want, my dear." He pulled his cravat straight, and then opened the door.

7

Wardour left the next day for Ashurst. He did not see Barbara before he went, but that morning an exquisite bouquet of hothouse flowers arrived for her. Robin, who had joined her for a late breakfast, quizzed her about them.

"Wardour has done everything to express his interest, but this is quite a floral tribute, Barb. Does this mean anything?"

"It does, Robin," she said with a smile.

Her brother set down his coffee cup and looked over at her, his eyebrows raised inquiringly.

"Peter and I became betrothed last night," she announced.

Delighted, Robin got up and went over to Barbara to give her a hug. Barbara felt tears come to her eyes as he pressed his cheek to hers. Robin was the person she felt closest to in the world. They might not have shared as many confidences as she had with her friends, but they had grown up supporting one another in the frequent absences of their parents.

Robin straightened up and cleared his throat. "I wish you happy, my dear. Diana and I have been concerned this past year that you would not be happy until you had a husband and family of your own, but there was no one before Wardour who seemed right for you. You do love him?"

"Yes, Robin," replied Barbara, after a slight hesitation.

"I know he does not come up to town for every Season.

Do you think you will be content living in Kent the year round? What of your music?"

"What of my music, Robin? I can take it no further. In some ways, living in London makes me more frustrated. I think I am ready to retire and play occasionally for family. And I am eager to be a mother," said Barbara, blushing a little.

"And one more along the lines of Judith than of our mother, I would bet," said her brother.

"Most definitely," agreed Barbara. "And since I do want to spend more time with my children, it is just as well that I relegate my music to a pastime. Motherhood is a realistic vocation; music could never be."

"Well, don't give it up entirely, Barbara," cautioned Robin. "You may be distracted by other things now, but it is very much a part of who you are."

"We shall see. Anyway," she continued, "Wardour is on his way to speak to Father today."

"You are lucky Peter proposed this week, then," joked her brother, "for he and Mother plan to leave for Scotland in a few days' time. I hope you can squeeze a betrothal party, not to mention your marriage, in between their jaunts."

Robin and Barbara looked at each other and laughed. They had long ago accepted the fact that their parents' devotion was reserved for each other. Much of their childhood had been spent awaiting the earl and countess's return from one or another of their trips, which seemed to function as perpetual honeymoons.

"You would think they would be content to remain at home now that they are older, Robin."

"I doubt they will ever change. And at this point, having Father around underfoot at Ashurst would be difficult. I have had things my way for the last few years because of his indifference, and I would resent any interference at this point."

"You and Diana have made it very much a home, Robin. Something it never was before. I appreciate that. In fact, I am looking forward to the end of the Season and a last summer in Ashurst."

"You have decided on a date?"

"Not yet. But I suspect Peter won't want to wait, so I think I will suggest a fall wedding."

Having announced her betrothal to Robin, Barbara was eager to tell Judith. She decided to forgo her morning ride, hoping that an early visit would find her friend alone. When she arrived, she was pleased to see that she had succeeded. Judith was in the library, her feet up on a footstool, reading the morning paper.

"Barbara! What a delightful surprise," she exclaimed, starting to get up.

"Don't disturb yourself, Judith," said Barbara.

"I am not that cumbersome yet, that I can't get up and greet a friend," protested the duchess.

"You look too comfortable to disturb."

"What brings you here this early in the day?" asked Judith, settling back against her cushion.

"I have some news that I wanted you to be the first to hear. Well, the second, since I announced it to Robin this morning."

"Wardour has proposed! And you . . .?"

"I have accepted."

"Oh, Barbara, I am so happy for you. Or, at least, I am if you indeed love him."

"I think I do," confessed Barbara, looking down at her feet in embarrassment.

"You think you do?" echoed Judith.

"I am sure I do. He is everything I could wish for: attentive, caring, an affectionate son and brother. We have been good friends from the first, but although friendship is a good basis for marriage, I wanted to be sure there could be more . . . and now that I am, I am looking forward to many years of happiness."

"Hmmm. And *how* do you know there could be more than friendship?" teased Judith.

"Last night he finally kissed me," announced Barbara.

"Only once?"

"There were a few kisses . . . very satisfactory kisses, I might add," Barbara told her. "I would not have said 'yes' otherwise. I have always held you and Simon up as my ideal. Most likely too high an ideal, or I might have accepted an offer before this. But I am very glad I waited."

"And have you set a date?"

"Not yet. He is off to Ashurst for my father's permission. I am hoping we both agree on a fall wedding."

"Promise me you won't have it before October in case the 'heir' is a bit late. Sophy kept us waiting for three weeks, if you remember."

"October it will be, if Peter is agreeable."

"He is not a frequent visitor to London. Do you think that will change?"

"I don't think so. And I am perfectly content with that, except for seeing my friends."

"We will just have to make sure we have several long visits a year. After all, Sutton is not that far from Arundel."

Judith ordered some lemonade and biscuits and they settled in for a cozy chat about wedding details. One thing was quickly settled: whatever the size of the celebration, Sophy would be a flower girl.

"She will be ecstatic," said Judith. "And it will keep her mind off the new baby and all the attention he will be receiving."

"You are so sure it is a 'he,' then?" teased Barbara.

"One does begin to form an attachment," replied Judith, passing her hand over her belly, "even when the baby is unseen. Simon very much wanted a girl the first time, and so we always thought of Sophy as a 'she.' This time, I am determined to get my way. And, of course, Simon wants an heir."

"I am hoping that by this time next year I will be an *enceinte* lady of leisure," said Barbara as she got up to leave.

Judith followed her to the door. "I wish you all the happiness that Simon and I have shared, my dearest friend," she said, squeezing Barbara's hands in hers. She had tears in her eyes as she waved Barbara down the street.

8

Since Wardour was not likely to return for a day or two, Barbara made plans to attend the theater with Viscount Vane and his wife and David Treves. The play was a comedy, and Barbara found herself laughing harder than she had in a long time, and indeed, the whole party was in a giddy mood as they made their way out of the theater.

Perhaps it was because they were distracted by their good humor, but it was not until they were almost upon it that they noticed the real-life drama occurring in front of them. Several young bucks, obviously the worse for a night of drinking, were gathered around one of the ever-present orange sellers. The hawker, an old man in a long black coat, was down on his hands and knees trying to retrieve his fruit, which was rolling around in front of him. Every time he had gathered a few up and replaced them in his basket, one of the young men would nudge the basket with his toe and upset it again. Two of the hawker's tormentors were tossing oranges back and forth, and dropping them in their drunken clumsiness. A small crowd of theatergoers stood around, enjoying the old man's confusion, and as Barbara drew closer, she could hear their taunts.

"Look at the Jew crawl," said one young woman, exquisitely gowned and coiffeured and with the ugliest expression on a beautiful face that Barbara had ever seen.

"Aye," said her escort, "let him beg for his 'gold' as I have had to beg for mine from his cousins, the cent-per-centers."

Barbara automatically put her hand out to stop David in the vain hope that he would not hear such filth. Sam was already among them, grabbing one drunk by his cravat and pushing him into another. They were too disoriented to put up a fight, and all was over in a few minutes. The spectators moved on and Sam helped the old man to his feet.

"Here is your basket," he said, placing its strap over the peddler's head. "We may be able to rescue some of this fruit." Nora and Sam got down on their hands and knees, picking up oranges and dusting them off, until the basket was at least one quarter full again.

David had not moved. Given the fact that most orange and lemon sellers were Jews, he had immediately guessed what was going on before he could even hear the drunken insults. He knew, of course, that incidents like this happened, but had never before been a witness to one. He had frozen in horror and distaste. Horror that human beings could be so cruel to one another. And, he had to admit, to his deep shame, distaste that the peddler and he shared something: not a religion or a way of life, but an identity that made them vulnerable to the most vile sort of persecution. He did not like being made to feel Jewish, and did not like himself for reacting that way.

By the time he was able to move, Sam was brushing off the old man's coat and asking him where he lived. "For we cannot let you go home alone tonight."

The peddler protested. "Thankee, sir, but there is no need. I am most grateful for your help, but I will get home with no trouble."

"Sam, someone must go with him," said Nora.

"I will." David felt shamed into taking some action. He had done nothing, stood by and watched, and now the viscount was prepared to go even further in an act of charity. "If you escort Lady Barbara, then I will make sure the old man gets home safely."

"Thank you, David," said Sam, and Barbara smiled at him with approval.

"Where do you live?" David asked the old man as the others moved off.

"Mitre Street."

David shuddered. Although Mitre Street was not in itself a bad street, their route lay through some of the worst slums in London. He grasped the peddler's arm and they started off.

David had not been in the heart of the East End before, but it was as bad as he could have imagined it: filthy, crowded, rat-infested, and crime-ridden. He did not relax until they had got to Mitre Street, something of an oasis in that it was cleaner and seemingly less populated than any street they had walked down so far.

"I live over there, sir," said the old man, pointing out a well-kept building bearing the sign "Jacob Cohen, Wholesale Fruit."

"Surely you are not Mr. Cohen?"

The old man gave a rasping sound which David took for a laugh. "No, no, sir. I'm Malachi Goldsmid. No relation, I hasten to add, to the better-known Goldsmid. No, Jacob is a kind man, a real 'Christian,' sir." Rasp, rasp. "I was dismissed from my tailoring position because my eyes were going, and he took pity on me. He sells me fruit cheaply, and lets me a room above his shop."

"Well, let us make sure someone is there tonight."

"Oh, yes, sir. Jacob and Deborah will be up doing the accounts, I have no doubt about it."

David pictured an older shopkeeper and his wife. When the door opened on the third knock, he was completely taken aback by the young woman framed in the doorway. She held a large candle, which illumined a pale face liberally covered with freckles and which set the tendrils of hair around her face on fire. It took David a minute to realize that she had red hair, glorious, thick red hair, which seemed to be alive and struggling to escape from the tight braid that hung over her shoulder.

"Excuse me, are you Mrs. Cohen?" asked David. He immediately heard Malachi's wheeze of a laugh behind him.

"I am Miss Cohen," replied the young woman. "What are you doing with Malachi?" she asked sharply, alarmed at the unlikely appearance of an exquisitely dressed gentleman at the door.

"There was an . . . incident in front of the theater tonight, and we felt he should not go home alone."

"An 'incident'? You mean some sort of attack, don't you? I am surprised that a fine gentleman like you would even care."

"Now, now, Miss Deborah," piped up Malachi. "No need for that. He's one of us."

"One of us?" she repeated skeptically.

"Mr. Goldsmid is correct. I am a Jew," admitted David.

Miss Cohen's expression did not alter at this revelation. She still looked doubtful.

"My name is David Treves. Or Tre-*ves* as my great-great grandfather would have pronounced it. I am Sephardic."

"That explains it, then," she said dismissively.

"Explains what?"

"Your clothes, your . . . fashionableness."

"There are many poor Sephardim, Miss Cohen."

"And you are certainly not one of them!"

Malachi had been listening to their exchange with great interest. There was a palpable energy between the two of them, and although negative, Deborah's response to Mr. Treves was the strongest reaction to a man he had ever seen from her. In his comings and goings as the Cohens' tenant, he had seen many young men become weary trying to spark a reaction from her. From what he had seen, she had responded to all with indifference. Until now.

"Mr. Tree-ves," said Malachi, falling somewhere between the old and new pronunciations, "must be a fine gentleman indeed, for he was with a party of real ladies and gentleman." The old peddler hoped this would impress Deborah.

It did, but not positively.

"So you are one of those Jews who try to pass as 'English gentlemen,'" she said with great contempt.

David was stung out of politeness. "It was one of those 'English gentlemen' who was the first to help Mr. Goldsmid. I am not sure where your so righteous anger comes from, Miss Cohen, but there are many good things to be said for an English gentleman."

"He's right, Miss Deborah. The young bucks that attacked me weren't real gentlemen. And I've had some Jews look right through me as if I weren't there. Not like Mr. Tree-ves here.

David was again ashamed of himself. He had been one of those Jews tonight, unwilling to be identified with someone who fit all of the stereotypes held by society. He wanted to be away from these streets, away from the old man, and most of all, away from Miss Cohen, whose scorn had not been tempered at all by Malachi's praises. The strength of his feelings surprised him.

"Mr. Goldsmid, now that I have seen you safely home, I will be on my way," he announced coolly. "Good evening, Miss Cohen. Perhaps we will meet again under better circumstances."

"Oh, I doubt that any business of yours will bring you back to Mitre Street."

"One never knows, does one?" replied David suavely. "After all, I could never have predicted this visit."

"Good night, Mr. Tree-ves," said Malachi.

"Good night, Mr. Goldsmid. I wish you good business to make up for tonight."

Deborah pulled the old man inside, and David heard her asking Malachi if he was sure he wasn't hurt as she closed the door behind them.

Deborah did not look back. If she had, she would have

seen David Treves standing there, wondering why, when only a few minutes ago he was in such a hurry to leave, he now didn't want to miss the last glimpse of Miss Cohen's red hair.

9

"It was quite painful to have David there as a witness," said Barbara the next morning, as she recounted the incident to Robin. "Do you think he is exposed to such scenes frequently?"

"I would not imagine he would have encountered much blatant hatred."

"Yet I have noticed a certain coldness, even rudeness, amongst members of society. In fact," continued Barbara with some hesitancy, "I do not think Diana entirely approves of my friendship with David."

Robin frowned, and Barbara hastened to add that she was making an observation, not a criticism.

"Oh, you need not apologize, Barb. You know that Diana comes from a fairly conservative family. In fact, I have always thought that her willingness to challenge the conventions when she was younger came from a need to proclaim her own independence rather than from any conviction. Once she had a family of her own, she settled down almost immediately," said Robin. "But many of the opinions that she holds are those she learned at home."

"Does that not bother you, Robin?" Barbara had been curious about this for years, but had never had such an appropriate opportunity to ask.

"Sometimes I envy the way Simon can open his mind to Judith. But a happy marriage need not depend on agreement on all particulars. In fact, I think some thrive on difference. When you marry Wardour, you will discover that, Barb, for the two of you are different in many ways."

"Yes, and there are times that I have worried about his being such a dyed-in-the-wool Tory. But he has a great deal of natural sympathy and common sense, and that more than makes up for his political leanings." Barbara was ready to continue when she saw their butler enter.

"Major Stanley."

"Yes, Henry?"

"The Marquess of Wardour is here." There was a faint trace of disapproval in his voice. It was clear that Henry thought such an early-morning visit the height of bad form.

"Send him in."

"I believe he wishes to see Lady Barbara, my lord."

"He must have gotten back from Ashurst late last night, and rushed over first thing. I hadn't thought him such a romantic," teased Robin.

"Show him into the drawing room, Henry," said Barbara, frowning at her brother. "I will be there directly."

"Bring him in for some refreshment after you have finished your billing and cooing."

Barbara crumpled her napkin and threw it at her brother, who expertly ducked and went on drinking his coffee. She was unaccountably nervous. She had accepted Wardour. There was no reason for her father to refuse him her hand, after all. So why did she have butterflies?

As soon as she opened the door and Wardour turned eagerly to meet her, all her nervousness fell away. He was the same familiar friend, amiable, handsome, and soon to be her husband.

"I am afraid your butler quite disapproves of me, Barbara, but I couldn't wait until a more fashionable hour."

"I am glad you didn't, Peter," said Barbara, extending her hands. "How was your visit to Ashurst?"

"As successful as I hoped it would be. Of course your father accepted my suit. So now we can make our betrothal official."

Barbara felt a momentary flash of annoyance, which she dismissed as irrational and unfair. There was no reason Wardour shouldn't have taken her father's approval for granted. What was there to object to? And by this time, her father would have been pleased to accept almost any eligible suitor. It was the unconscious self-satisfaction in Wardour's voice that bothered her.

"I will have Robin contact the *Times* immediately," replied Barbara. "And the *Post*."

A slight frown creased Wardour's forehead at the thought of his name appearing in a liberal newspaper, but he forgot everything as Barbara stepped closer and lifted her face up for a kiss.

Their kiss was deep and slow, a fitting seal to their official betrothal. Wardour was the first to pull away, to Barbara's disappointment.

"We must be careful of being alone these next few months, my dear. It is hard to treat you with the respect I feel for you."

"Oh, I think it is allowable, now that we are betrothed, to have the balance fall in favor of passionate kisses rather than respectful embraces," said Barbara teasingly.

Wardour smiled down at her. "That is what attracted me to you in the first place," he told her. "Your spirited nature. I am a trifle too reserved, perhaps."

Somehow, Wardour managed to say this in such a way that Barbara felt mildly criticized rather than complimented, and Wardour sounded satisfied with himself despite his self-depreciation. But their kiss had been more than satisfactory, and so she dismissed her slight apprehension.

"Come, Robin bade me bring you to the breakfast table."

"I am a bit hungry," admitted her fiancé. "I came immediately, and have had nothing to eat since last night."

Such evidence of loverly impatience erased all of Barbara's momentary annoyance.

Robin rose when they entered and shook Wardour's hand. "I assume you had no difficulty with my father?"

"No, no, Lord Ashurst was everything that is pleasant. He did not challenge me at all. In fact, he seemed a bit blasé about my qualifications," concluded Wardour on a puzzled note.

Robin and Barbara laughed. "You must realize, Wardour," said Robin, "that our parents' main interest and concern is for one another."

Wardour started to protest. "Indeed, I would not presume to criticize . . ."

"No need to apologize. Father is well aware of your eligibility, and I'm sure well-pleased with your suit. He was probably distracted by plans for their trip to Scotland."

"I suppose I assumed that all parents are like my mother, who is devoted to my interests," apologized Wardour. "Of course, if my father were still alive, things would no doubt be different."

"Please do not concern yourself, Peter," chimed in Barbara. "Now, make yourself comfortable and I will fix you a plate. We like to breakfast in private, so there is no footman to serve you."

Just as Barbara placed a plate of eggs and kidneys in front of Wardour, Henry appeared again.

"Sir David Treves is here, my lady. I believe you were engaged to ride together this morning."

"Oh, goodness, I completely forgot! Please send him in. We ride together once a week, you know, Peter," explained Barbara. "We have become great friends."

Wardour, of course, had been aware of their acquaintance, since Treves had been present occasionally at routs and musicales. He had not realized the extent of their intimacy, however, and did not really approve of the future Marchioness of Wardour having a close friendship with a Jew, but this was clearly not the time and place to discuss the issue. He was everything that was agreeable and polite when David was shown in.

"I apologize for my buckskins," David immediately announced.

"Nonsense. I apologize for my absent-mindedness," said Barbara. "But I do have an excuse," she continued. "You are one of the first to hear of my official betrothal to Peter."

"My best wishes to both of you," said David, with a warm smile for Barbara.

"Please join us," insisted Robin.

"Just for a moment or two. I do not wish to intrude." David was very good, as indeed he had had to be, at detecting the subtlest disapproval. There was only a bit of tension emanating from Wardour, but David picked it up, if the Stanleys hadn't.

"You must tell me what happened after we left you last night, David. We were witnesses to an incident of cruelty to an old peddler," she explained to Wardour. "David was kind enough to escort him home."

"The old man was only shaken, and I was able to get him home with no problems at all. He lives above a fruiterer's on Mitre Street," David added.

"Mitre Street! I don't know the city all that well, but surely that is the East End and full of riffraff and criminals?" exclaimed Wardour.

You mean to say Jewish riffraff, I am sure, thought David.

"It *is* a crowded and poor area," he admitted.

"Was there someone to take care of him?" asked Barbara.

"As a matter of fact, I left him in the capable hands of Miss Deborah Cohen, the daughter of the owner."

"Good. I was worried about the aftereffects of the shock."

"Old Malachi is tougher than he looks," said David. "But enough of my adventure. When is the wedding to be?"

"In the fall. At least, that is what I would wish, but we have not had much time to discuss details."

"First you must come to Arundel for an extended visit,

my dear. I want you to get to know my mother better and see the household to plan for any changes you might like to make."

"I would love to do that, Peter," said Barbara gratefully. "Although I am not one of those women who feels she must go changing everything around. I am sure your home is lovely already."

"I was hoping you might come for a July visit."

"That would be perfect," exclaimed Barbara. "That way I would not miss the Midsummer Fair at Ashurst. With Mother and Father away so often, Robin and I have got into the habit of representing them. It is rather a tradition."

"July it is, then," said Wardour. "And now I must go. I will see you tonight, my dear, at the Rosses' ball?"

"I am looking forward to our waltz," said Barbara. "Let me walk with you to the door."

"I am of a mind to send Treves with you as a chaperon," teased Robin.

"Oh, no, I do not believe in cramping a betrothed couple's style," David responded.

Wardour frowned slightly at the jests, but Barbara's laugh restored his good humor. And it was true that he fully intended to have another kiss before he left.

10

The Stanleys' last days in London passed quickly and happily for Barbara. The official announcement of her betrothal gave her friends and acquaintances great pleasure and also the excuse to hold the additional Venetian breakfast or small supper dance to celebrate. Barbara enjoyed them all, although by the time they were to leave for Ashurst, she was looking forward to the slower pace of country life.

The Stanleys reached Sussex well before the Midsummer Fair. Diana, who had been busy with the twins for the past few years, had never become involved except to put in the expected attendance at the Ashurst picnic and a few hours at the fair itself.

Robin and Barbara, however, were much busier. "After all," Robin had joked once, "We must act *in loco parentis,* and Barbara had joined him in helpless laughter at the image. At the time, Diana had thought that the here-again, gone-again life of the earl and his countess was nothing to joke about. Her own parents had always been present, responsible, and quite strict with all their offspring, a fact that had allowed her to comfortably rebel at the appropriate time and then settle into model wife and motherhood. She rather resented the fact that so much was expected of Robin before he had even inherited the title. But she was relieved, she had to confess to herself, that Barbara was willing, nay, enjoyed taking her mother's place at the fair.

It was tradition that the Stanleys host a picnic open to everyone in the neighborhood the day before the fair opened. Much of Barbara's time was spent planning the food and drinks for over a hundred people, making sure that the long trestle tables and benches were carried down from the barn and wiped clean of spiderwebs and checked for hornets' nests. One unforgettable year, a swarm of wasps had constructed their nest under one of the tables. The servants had not noticed the papery gray structure under the legs of the table, since the tables had grayed over the years and the nest was almost indistinguishable. At any rate, Squire Pike and his lady, both a bit overweight and notoriously slow-moving, were stung, quite literally, into movement resembling a St. Vitus's dance. When they were finally calmed down and the cause of their jumping and slapping at themselves and each other was discovered, one of the old women from the village called for "mud, mud!" and managed to plaster them both to her satisfaction, if not to theirs. Robin had disgraced himself. Normally abstemious, he always overindulged in the home-brewed ale at the picnic, and he was rolling on the ground at the sight of the mud-caked squire. He laughed so hard and so long that the next morning, when Barbara scolded him for insulting the Pikes, his stomach was actually sorer than his head.

While Barbara kept herself busy with the picnic, Robin was involved with the village planning committee. Every year for the past twenty, the vicar had protested the "pagan" custom of Midsummer's Eve, when a huge bonfire was lit on Ashurst Hill and flaming cartwheels of bound straw and pitch were rolled down toward the village. And every year he was voted down by farmers and townsmen alike, who might have forgotten the origins of this time-honored ritual, but who *knew*, if the wheels were still burning at the bottom of the hill, there would be a good harvest. Robin always voted with the villagers, for when he was a child his father had allowed him to stay up late on Midsummer's Eve, and the sight of the flames reaching up to the heavens and then apparently giving birth to small, rolling fires had not only been one of the thrills of his boyhood but, he knew, had deepened his commitment to the land. He had learned to live with the vicar's short-lived disappointment in him, for he was, after all, a regular churchgoer and the family a generous contributor to the upkeep of St. Thomas's. But the celebration of the turning of the wheel of the year pulled at something very deep in him.

Once the question of the bonfire was settled, the meeting always went smoothly. There would be the agricultural competitions, of course, and piemen and jugglers and a gypsy fortune-teller. The vicar didn't waste his breath protesting this, for he knew that Madame Zenobia was the most popular attraction and drew in every young woman, common or gentry, to have her palm read or Tarot cards interpreted. A Punch and Judy show was a welcome addition this year. And, of course, there was always music and dancing.

"There is a young fiddler I heard when I went to market last month," announced the squire, "and I was so impressed that I made sure to invite him. I assured him that he would make as much or more money in Ashurst as anywhere else, and perhaps might be hired to play for the country dancing." He looked questioningly at Robin.

"If old Daniel does not mind sharing the limelight, I am sure we can support another fiddler. He must be talented for you to go out of your way to invite him, Joseph."

"I confess I surprised myself. I have never done more than toss a coin at a busker, certainly never talked to one. But he kept my toes tapping with his reels and almost brought tears to my eyes with his slow tunes."

"I will make sure to tell Barbara to look for him," Robin said. "How might she recognize him?"

"Oh, surely by his music," the squire replied. "But you

can't miss him by his appearance. He is a tall, bearded Scot."

"Well, he should be easy enough to find," said Robin with a smile. "I will tell Barbara to keep her eyes and ears open."

11

Ashurst celebrated Midsummer's Eve on June 22 instead of the old date of July 4, and the vicar, of course, insisted on referring to it as St. John's Eve, to give the rituals a semblance of respectability. All morning the young men and boys were busy dragging wood up Ashurst Hill, while the old men bound the straw cartwheels.

Most of the women were busy putting the finishing touches on their best dresses. Half of the ribbon sold in the village went for decorating clothes and hair. The other half ended up on the old thorn tree that stood on the edge of the village green. By midday, it was almost hidden under the flowers and ribbons that adorned it.

Barbara had not a moment to spare, since she was taking care of all the last-minute arrangements for the picnic. There had been a few small catastrophes, like the youngest kitchen maid adding salt instead of sugar to the whipping cream, and the lugubrious appearance of the cook, who against all practical considerations had become attached to the young rooster that was first to be killed that morning.

"He always ate the corn right out of me hand," she kept saying, until the rest of the kitchen staff were ready to put *her* head on the chopping block.

Despite that and the fact that one of the young lads had mistaken a nettle patch for the herb garden, and there was now one less pair of hands to move furniture, all went smoothly. "Or as smoothly as can be expected," muttered

Barbara, who had just heard some commotion by the kitchen door.

When she went to investigate, she discovered that Madame Zenobia had decided (or perhaps it was the stars that had decided, Barbara wasn't quite sure) that she should begin her readings at the picnic. It was impossible to convince the old gypsy that her presence wasn't required till the morrow, and Barbara finally gave in, telling her that she could join the picnic and set up at one of the tables when supper was over. And no, there would be no pentangled-bedecked tent set up on the grounds of Ashurst, thank you. The cook and the kitchen maids were ecstatic at the compromise, for they had been promised the first readings. And the old woman thanked Barbara profusely, and pulled something green out of her pocket.

"Here, my lady, this is especially for you, for your kindness to a helpless old woman."

A less helpless old woman Barbara had never seen. She was a shrewd bargainer and had got her way after all, so Barbara had to hide a smile at the obsequious tone in Madame Zenobia's voice as she presented what appeared to be a sprig of myrtle. Indeed, the old woman herself had a self-mocking twinkle in her eye.

"I have seen that you have a lover, my lady."

Barbara looked around to see if Wardour had somehow appeared to surprise her.

"I see it in the cards, my lady, in the cards."

Well, anyone in the village could have told her, thought Barbara. There was no magic in this.

"Now, if ye wishes to find out if this lover will marry you, then tonight, before you go to bed, put this sprig of myrtle in your prayer book."

Barbara chuckled. "We are formally betrothed, Madame Zenobia, so there is no doubt in my mind about the marriage."

"You may laugh, but much can happen between a betrothal and a marriage. Now, you must put this myrtle upon the words from the marriage ceremony. Then close your book and put it under the pillow you sleep on."

"And how will I know if my fiancé will indeed become my husband?"

"If the myrtle is gone in the morning, then you know that both of you will remain faithful. But if the myrtle is still there in your prayer book, then he will never marry you."

"It seems rather a dangerous test, Madame Zenobia. I would rather it were the other way around. For it is most likely that the myrtle will not go anywhere overnight!"

"Just do as I say, my lady, and you will have an answer in the morning."

Barbara put the myrtle in her pocket and, thanking the old woman, got back to work. A good old-fashioned way of keeping young maidens in line, she thought. For, of course, the myrtle would always be there in the morning and would keep the young women from parting with their virtue too easily and trusting the easy promises of a lover.

The picnic was a great success, as it was every year. Everyone mingled, regardless of rank, and by the time the toasts were drunk, all, particularly the men, were flushed with good spirits.

The light lingered and prolonged the festivities, for to-morrow was the longest day of the year. By the time the sun went down, the men were a bit more sober.

"Thank God," said Barbara to Robin as they watched the villagers set off to light the fire on the hill. "I always worry that someone will be so drunk that he will fall in and do his jumping over flames instead of ashes."

"Someday I should go leaping over the fire," Robin said, as he did every year.

"You know that this is their part of the feast, Robin. And with twins, you hardly need worry about fertility!"

"For shame, Barbara," teased her brother. "You know it is to increase the harvest yield."

"Ah, so you always say, but it seems to me that too many

young girls are increasing after Midsummer's Eve. Perhaps old Zenobia's myrtle sprig is a good custom."

"What's that?"

Barbara pulled the myrtle out of her pocket, where it had lain forgotten till now. "I am to put this in my prayer book, and if I sleep on it and it is still there in the morning, then I will know that Peter will not marry me."

"I dare you to do it," Robin challenged, with a gleam in his eye.

"I cannot accept such a challenge, Robin, for we both know it will be there in the morning."

"Aren't you sure of Wardour?" Robin said with a smile.

"Of course I am. And even if the myrtle were still there, it would mean nothing. It is only an old superstition. But I am not afraid to take your dare."

"Done," said her brother, who had decided that if Barbara accepted, he would steal into her room and remove the sprig himself. He wanted nothing to mar her happiness with Wardour. She was a very intelligent young woman, his sister, but all women had an irrational streak in them, and now that he had pushed her to it, he didn't want her to have even a fleeting disappointment.

When Barbara got to her bedchamber, she opened her prayer book, found the marriage service, and carefully placed the myrtle on the right words, then put the prayer book under her pillow.

It will be there in the morning, of course, she thought. And Robin and I will laugh at ourselves, for it will mean nothing.

Unfortunately, when Robin went to bed a few hours later, he was so sleepy from the ale he had consumed and his vigil, watching till the fire burned down, that he completely forgot his plan and fell asleep immediately.

And when Barbara awoke in the morning, conscious of a strange lump under her pillow, she almost didn't open the book, saying to herself, I know it will be there, and I know it doesn't mean anything that it is. Yet she couldn't resist.

And there it was, the dark green leaves flattened and dried out. She suffered a momentary pang of doubt, and then, laughing at herself, closed the prayer book. "Let the myrtle stay," she said aloud. "And when we are married, I will open this and show Peter and we will have a good laugh."

12

After all their work on the picnic, the Stanleys usually relaxed in the morning and made their appearance at the fair in the afternoon. This year, they didn't set out until after two o'clock, all crowded into the old landau: Barbara, Robin, Diana, the twins, and the twins' nurse. As they drove through town the noise and dust became more noticeable and by the time they were dropped off, the twins were beside themselves with excitement.

Robin was one of the judges at the cattle show, and he was off quickly, leaving the women together. Barbara traditionally awarded the prize for the best domestic animal, but that wasn't until later in the afternoon, and so she spent some time with Diana and the children, buying lemonade and sweets, keeping them out of the freak-show tent ("For surely," said Diana, "they are too young for a two-headed calf, much less the Cotswold Giant. I do not want them having nightmares"). The Punch and Judy show was perfect, and so when Diana decided to stay through a second performance, Barbara, having arranged a meeting place, wandered off on her own. Robin had mentioned the new fiddler to her, and as she walked, she had her ears open. She came across several buskers, one with a tin whistle and one with a fiddle, but the fiddler was small, dark, and English, and not that memorable a musician. She was beginning to wonder if the Scotsman had got to the fair when she heard the strains of a reel and followed the sound to its source.

There was a fair crowd around the musician, so that Barbara could only see the top of his head, bent down over his bow. As soon as people saw her they cleared a space, and she found herself right in front of him.

He was tall, auburn-haired, and bearded. He was playing a fiddle that looked as old and worn as his clothes. His eyes were almost closed and his whole body moved in time to the music. It seemed as though the instrument was an extension of his body, not separate from him, and the music emerged from his whole self. Barbara had always enjoyed dance tunes, but she had never been particularly impressed by a popular musician before. The tunes were usually only background music for dancing, and as good as old Daniel was, he could not hold a candle to this young Scotsman.

It was no problem identifying him as a Scot, thought Barbara, as she glanced at the worn kilt that swayed and swung out with his hips. His legs were covered with the same reddish hair as was on his head and chin. I shouldn't be looking at his legs, she scolded herself. But I have never seen this much of a man's legs before!

The tune ended, which startled Barbara out of her next thought, which was the age-old question of what Scotsmen wore under their kilts. When she looked up, she found herself looking into a pair of bright blue eyes, one of which slowly and deliberately closed in a decided wink, as though the fiddler knew exactly what she was thinking.

He must have just finished a set of tunes, for most of the people around her were throwing money into the old bonnet in front of him and moving off, leaving her as his only audience.

"And are ye not going to drop some silver into ma' wee bonnet, lassie?" he inquired with a grin.

His Scottish burr was as broad as Barbara had expected.

"Perhaps another tune will make you smile and open your purse. I usually wait for more of a crowd, but I will play this one just for you."

Barbara knew she should have turned on her heel and

left. It was very clear from her appearance that she was a lady, and although she was not overly conscious of rank, neither was she used to being treated with such boldness. On the other hand, there was such good humor about it that she could not work herself up into feeling offended. And as soon as the bow touched the strings, she was rooted to the spot. He played a slow air for her, and nothing she had ever heard, not even Mozart, had moved her as much. It was a simple sweet tune, speaking as directly and clearly to her as a bird on a bright spring morning.

When the music ended, they both stood quietly for a moment as though not to break a spell. Barbara knew that his was a great talent, and thought what a pity it was that he was uneducated and untrained.

She smiled up at him. "You were right. That tune would cause a miser's fist to open like a baby's hand. Here," she said, as she pulled a small purse from her reticule and handed him a guinea.

She was embarrassed almost as soon as she did it. She should have just dropped a few silver coins in his bonnet like everyone else. Instead, here she was, clearly pointing out the difference in rank by being overly generous.

"Gold, my lady? Thankee, thankee. This will keep me for a good fortnight." He sounded both mocking and grateful, and she blushed.

"You have a genuine talent, sir. I only meant to acknowledge it."

"Aye, and you did it right generously. Dinna fash yourself, lass."

"'Dinna fash myself'?" repeated Barbara.

"Do not get yourself into a taking over it, my lady," he replied in perfect English.

"I think I prefer the Scots way," said Barbara.

"Oh, aye, one word can sometimes convey a lot." His burr was as broad again as ever.

Another audience had begun to gather behind her, so

Barbara had no time to comment on the changes in his accent. Not that it is any business of mine, she thought, as she moved off. But it was interesting that for a moment he sounded like an educated man.

13

It was lucky that Barbara was not missish, for judging the domestic-pet competition often meant holding toads and snakes as well as petting the occasional brute of a mastiff. As a judge, she had to have not only strong nerves but the wisdom of Solomon and the political savvy of a Parliament member. As in any small village, there were popular and unpopular citizens and very long memories. In 1803, for instance, Miss Heath had won first prize for her pet duck and won again in 1807 and 1815. No matter how handsome her drake was this year (and he was a fine specimen), Barbara would not dare award her first prize. The Widow Claff's pet parrot had won only two years ago, despite his outrageous language. In fact, Barbara counted herself lucky that she had only been called an "ould tart," which was a mild insult compared to others she had heard from the parrot. Luckily, the bird was getting old and mangy, thought Barbara as she passed by his cage. She could pass him by this year without guilt.

There was the usual assortment of puppies and kittens. There were also two hedgehogs and one pet pig, which Barbara thought made for good variety. Jimmy George brought the annual garter snake and his brother a pet mouse. Barbara knew both boys well enough to realize that they were hoping this year they'd succeed in making her scream or at least give a little jump. But she had grown up with an older brother who had been known to drop caterpillars down her dress, so she had no problem appearing genuinely appreciative of Albert, the white mouse.

The last pet she came to was Betsy Landon's. Barbara had always loved Betsy, who was a shy, sweet child. She lived with her mother and father on a small farm, and Barbara assumed that the box sitting in front of her contained a chick or a duckling, and so she picked it up and opened it nonchalantly, ready to exclaim in delight over a fluffy-feathered baby.

What she saw was a black, hairy, giant spider. She screeched and dropped the box, and Jimmy told his parents later that it was the best fair he could remember for years. Luckily, although the spider had fallen out of the box, it did not go anywhere, but lifted itself on its hind legs as though ready to attack.

"Barnabas won't hurt you, Lady Barbara, he is really very tame," said Betsy, reaching down and picking up her "pet." She placed the spider on her palm and gently stroked him. "See, you can even pet him."

Barbara would have felt thoroughly humiliated had the whole audience not moved back a few feet to escape the menacing beast. But she was embarrassed to have been frightened by a creature that an eight-year-old was holding so calmly, so she reached out her hand and touched Barnabas with the tips of her fingers.

"Wherever did you find Barnabas?" she asked.

"Oh, I didn't find him, my lady. My uncle Matt brought him for me. He's a sailor, you know."

"I presume you mean your Uncle Matt and not Barnabas," said a familiar voice from behind Barbara. She turned and saw the Scots fiddler.

Betsy's face lit up at the joke. "Perhaps Barnabas could be called a sailor too, for he sailed all the way from South America in a cargo ship. My uncle found him when they were unloading bananas. He eats rotten fruit, you know."

"Your Uncle Matt?" replied the Scotsman with mock horror.

Betsy giggled. "No, no, you great silly, *Barnabas*. We always make sure he has some old fruit or vegetable to nibble on. He's a tran . . . ta-ran-tu-la," she pronounced carefully and proudly. "My Uncle Matt says he *could* bite and poison someone if you wanted him to," she continued a bit fiercely, holding the spider out toward Jimmy, who had crept back to get a closer look. Jimmy was the bane of her existence because of his teasing, and Betsy took great pleasure in seeing the fear on his face as he stepped backward again.

"Aye, it is good to have a friend like Barnabas, lassie, said the Scotsman, smiling down at her.

"And he is a fine-looking specimen of his breed," said Barbara. She turned around and announced to everyone who remained that she had never seen such an excellent tarantula and it was clear to her that Barnabas had won first prize. And that is no lie, she thought to herself, for since none of us has seen such a creature, there can be no complaints or comparisons.

Betsy's face lit up and her hand trembled as she accepted the blue ribbon and the guinea that were first prize. She popped Barnabas back in his box and went off to find her parents.

"Well done, my lady," said the fiddler.

"Why are you here, sir, and not off somewhere playing your fiddle?" demanded Barbara.

"I am a great animal lover," he explained, his eyes twinkling. "And I remember the pet competitions when I was a boy. It takes great diplomacy to be the judge. I would say that the Old Bailey is all the poorer that women cannot sit on the bench!"

"Enough of your toadying, Mr. . . .?"

"Alec Gower." Alec had borrowed his teacher's surname for the year.

"Good day, Mr. Gower," said Barbara, turning on her heel and trying to keep a dismissive tone in her voice. He was encroaching, this fiddler. But there was something about the man . . . His talent, for one thing. And his charm. He had been utterly charming with Betsy.

Alec watched Barbara walk off. A fine-looking woman, lad, he said to himself. Oh, aye, and it is too bad ye canna expect her to gie ye a second look. For the first time since he had left his grandfather's library, he chafed under the conditions of their wager. Lady Barbara was clearly related to the Earl of Ashurst, whether his sister or daughter. As the grandson of the Duke of Strathyre, he would have been able to pursue an acquaintance. As a poor wandering musician, he was beneath her notice. But she had noticed his music, by God, and this evening he would make sure she noticed it again.

The dancing was held on the village green, with a temporary platform erected for the musicians. Old Daniel had been a bit resentful at first at the stranger's presence, but after he had heard him play, his envy melted away. Gower's talent was far superior to any of Daniel's rivals in Sussex or Kent. They played together and then each played a few dances alone. Daniel's music, as always, was a joy to dance to. But when Gower played, something magical seemed to happen. Everyone felt more energy; the figures of the dances flowed together, one into the other, so that no step felt separate. The dancers, the dance, and the music were as one.

There was no attention paid to rank on Midsummer Day. All danced together: Robin with the blacksmith's wife, the squire with his tenant's mother, and Barbara with Betsy's father. And so when the fiddler approached her, she shouldn't have been surprised.

"May I have this dance, Lady Barbara?" he asked in un-accented English.

Barbara was flustered, but could hardly refuse him. Daniel struck up a reel, so there was little chance for exchanging pleasantries, even if she could have thought of any. Despite his height, Gower was a graceful dancer, and once she had given herself over to the music she realized she had never had such a sympathetic partner. There was a smile on her face by the end of the tune that she couldn't have hidden if she had wanted to. And somewhere, deep inside her, she felt a stirring of joy. She had almost forgotten, in the disappointments of the past few years, what that felt like.

"Ye have a fine pair of legs for dancing, lass."

"Tell me, Mr. Gower, how is it that sometimes you speak the King's English, and at other times you are almost incomprehensible?" asked Barbara, ignoring his outrageous compliment.

"I went to a hard school, lassie, wi' a master who tried to beat the Scots out of me." Which was not too far from the truth, thought Alec. His grandfather had never approved of Alec's mother, and strictly forbade any lapse into Scots. "Ye might say I can speak like a Sassenach, but Scots is ma mither tongue. And have ye recovered from yoor wee fright this afternoon?" he continued, a wicked grin on his face.

"What fright, Barbara?" asked Robin, who had wandered over to compliment the fiddler on his playing.

"The winner of the pet show was a huge hairy spider, Robin."

Robin gave a shout of laughter. "Did you disgrace yourself? My sister has bravely faced snakes and toads, but she hates spiders," he explained to Alec.

"This is my brother, Major Stanley," said Barbara. "Mr. Gower. My brother was the first to discover my fear of spiders," she explained. "I got used to almost everything else he tormented me with, but never spiders."

"It is a small failing, Lady Barbara. And you rose above it bravely today," Alec continued with mock gallantry. He had thought the major her brother from the striking resemblance. And he had checked her left hand during their dance, so she must be the earl's daughter, he thought. Though what possible relevance that could hold for Alec Gower, fiddler, he didn't know.

"I think Daniel is ready for a glass of ale, Gower," said Robin. "He is waving you over, and looks quite desperate."

Alec gave a slight bow to Barbara, thanked her for the reel, and ran up to the platform, his kilt swinging.

"The squire was right. He is an extraordinary musician, don't you think, Barb?"

It took Barbara a moment to reply, for she was thinking more about his dancing and how wonderful it had felt to have him swing her around. The little bubble of joy was still with her. "Yes, Robin, yes. Extraordinary."

14

The next morning, despite all her activity over the past few days, Barbara was up before anyone else. There was an early-morning mist hanging over the fields, and she tried to stay in bed and finish the novel she had been reading, but for some reason she was too restless to concentrate. She finally threw her book down and decided to go for a ride.

It was a magical time to be out, for this early it felt as if the whole world were sleeping except for herself. With the mist swirling around her, Barbara followed the track alongside the wheat fields, enjoying a slow canter for almost a mile. There was a small copse at the end of the Ashurst fields, separating them from the squire's property, and as she got closer to the trees, she began to sniff the air. She must be imagining things, probably because she hadn't yet had breakfast, but she could swear she smelled bacon. The closer she got to the copse, the stronger the smell, and she decided that she was not hallucinating; some gypsy or tramp on Ashurst land, she thought, with a trace of annoyance. It was customary to ask permission, which the Stanleys usually granted, particularly after the Midsummer Fair. She would inform whoever this was that he was trespassing.

She ducked her head as her horse moved through the small grove of trees, and was almost upon the little camp before she knew it. There was Mr. Gower, smiling up at her in delighted surprise.

"Had I known you were coming for breakfast, my lady, I would have thrown a few more slices on the pan."

He hadn't even gotten up, thought Barbara, but was sitting there for all the world as though she were the trespasser. With his shirt wide open, exposing the reddish hair on his chest and his kilt pulled up over his knees. How in the world did Scottish women keep their minds off men's bodies? It was hard to ignore them, with so much of them showing. And what if there was nothing beneath his kilt . . . ?"

"We have no objection to the occasional traveler," said Barbara, "but it is customary to ask permission to camp at Ashurst."

"Oh, is this still Stanley land, Lady Barbara? I must have mistaken the boundaries. The squire told me I could camp as long as I liked. I'll move, if you wish, but not until I've had my breakfast, if you don't mind."

The fiddler was speaking neither broad Scots nor "proper" English, but something in between. The light burr sounded natural, whereas his other accents had seemed exaggerations.

"No, there is no need to 'fash' yourself," said Barbara. "Not that you seem easily 'fashed'!"

"Ah, weel, what is a few feet more or less, lassie? Now come down off your high horse and have some breakfast with me."

Since her gelding *was* over sixteen hands, Barbara supposed the description was accurate, but she knew quite well that was not the way he had meant it. She couldn't help smiling at the rogue, however, for he was charming. And Lord, the bacon smelled wonderful and she was hungry.

She dismounted and tied her horse to a tree. The Scotsman was sitting in the middle of a long fallen tree, but he moved down and patted the space next to him. "This will be more comfortable than the ground, lassie, which is still a bit damp. I should know"—he grinned, rubbing his hip—"for I've been sleeping on it."

Barbara sat, but left a good foot between herself and the fiddler.

"The bacon is almost ready. And I've got two eggs and a half a loaf of bread. I did well at the fair."

"Do you always sleep outdoors, Mr. Gower?" Barbara asked, wondering for the first time what it would be like to earn one's living on the road.

"When it is not cold or rainy I do. Too many comfortable nights in an inn and I might go hungry for a day or two." Alec slid an egg and a few slices of bacon onto a battered tin plate and passed it to Barbara. There was an old coffeepot sitting almost in the fire, and he filled an equally battered cup with the strong liquid.

"Ye'll have to forgive me, lass, for eating wi' ma fingers, but I hae only one knife and fork, alas."

"There you go again, with that exaggerated accent."

"Ach, I canna resist it. The sight of ye there, wi' the mist in yer hair and yer cheeks flushed wi' exercise, and yer red rosy lips wi' a bit of egg clinging to them just soften ma tongue, lassie."

Before Barbara could move, Alec had reached out and gently removed the offending piece of egg with his finger, licking it off afterward.

"You are incorrigible, Mr. Gower. Quite lacking in respect." Barbara tried to keep her tone stern, but that bubble of joy, which had shrunk a bit overnight, was expanding again. She gave in to it and laughed. "I suppose that such a practiced charm is necessary in your business. I just cannot believe how easy it is to succumb to it. But I am surprised. I had heard that the Scots were dour and serious creatures."

"Aye, some of our Presbyterian brethren gie us a bad name. But not all of us are life-hating."

"You seem to thoroughly enjoy life, though yours must be a hard one."

"I do, Lady Barbara, I do," said Gower with great seriousness and a touch of wonder. "Much more than I thought I would have," he added, almost to himself.

"Of course, you have your music. You are lucky to make your art your life," said Barbara a bit wistfully.

"You sound a wee bit envious, lass."

"I suppose I am. I am a musician myself, but I shall never be able to do anything serious with it."

"You play the fortepiano?"

"It is either that or the harp for a gentlewoman, isn't it? The fortepiano. But I have given up playing for the last few months. It seems pointless."

"Doing something you love is never pointless, my lady."

"That is an admirable philosophy, Mr. Gower, but hard to live up to. And anyway, after I am married, I will be too busy." Barbara wasn't sure why she had revealed so much of herself, but in addition to his easy charm, Gower had an air of sympathy about him.

"And are you to be married soon, Lady Barbara?"

"In the fall I will wed Peter Rushcliffe, Marquess of Wardour." Giving his full title seemed to emphasize the social distance between them, something Barbara needed to do. She was feeling too comfortable with Gower.

"And does the marquess not appreciate your talent?" he asked quietly.

"Actually, although he was always quite complimentary whenever I played for him last year, I do not think he has a great feeling for music himself," confessed Barbara.

Alec silently wished her well. He knew how lonely it was to have no one in your immediate family understand your greatest love. He had no idea what Wardour was like, but doubted that any gentleman would want his wife to have a consuming interest in anything but running his household and raising his children.

The sun was burning off the mist and a shaft of light shone down through the trees, so that all was green and sparkling. For a moment the copse was an enchanted place, quite set apart from everyday life and its rigid conventions. Alec murmured something that sounded like "And all comes down to a green thought in a green shade," and Barbara's eyes opened in surprise to hear a traveling fiddler quote Marvell. But the outside world seemed so distant that she didn't want to break the spell to satisfy her curiosity.

The sound of her horse's soft whickering brought her back to herself.

"I must go, Mr. Gower, before my horse takes off by himself and before the family begins to worry about me. Thank you for the breakfast, and good luck on your travels."

Once again Alec regretted his wager. Not that revealing himself would have achieved anything, he thought, as he watched Barbara bring her horse over to the log to mount. She was already betrothed, and sounded very content with her marquess.

Barbara mounted quickly so that the Scotsman would have no chance to offer any help. Just the gentle brushing of egg from her lips had affected her more than Wardour's most passionate kiss, and she didn't want to be making any more comparisons.

She arrived home as Robin and Diana were coming down to breakfast, and excused herself to change from her riding habit. When she came down to the table, Robin was curious that her ride had not seemed to stimulate her appetite, but Barbara excused the solitary muffin on her plate by saying that she had eaten far too much at the fair and would probably have no appetite for days.

The next morning she rose early and rode again, telling herself it had been such a lovely ride the day before and that she merely wanted the exercise. She rode the same way, but this time, when she approached the copse, there was no smell of bacon, and when she got to the small clearing, no fire and no Gower. She breathed a sigh of relief and disappointment. She had enjoyed her conversation with the fiddler, but she was an engaged woman, and surely should not be drawn to another man, particularly one not of her class. She was unlikely ever to see him again, she thought, and turned her horse toward Ashurst and away from the distracting memories of those bright blue eyes and contagious good humor. In a few days' time she would be getting ready for her visit to Arundel and her first introduction to what would be her new life.

15

While his friends and acquaintances in society retired to their estates in the country, David Treves remained in London. Business did not come to a halt with the end of a Season, and so the Treves town house remained open all year. On the most stifling days, David and his father were able to refresh themselves, however, with an overnight visit to the family home in Surrey.

Until he had escorted old Malachi home, David had not given much thought to the condition of the poor, Jewish or otherwise. Although he shared a general interest in reform with men like Viscount Vane and the Duke of Sutton, he had not been as concerned with the lot of the common people as he was with beginning to stimulate interest in political emancipation for the Jews. He wanted to win for other young men the possibilities that had not been open for him: entry into university, Parliament, or the Inns of Court. He was in the minority, both in society and at home, however, for many Jews were silent and apathetic, having no desire to take part in politics. Life in England was easier than on the Continent, where all Jews had to struggle for survival, and most of David's well-to-do friends were content with things the way they were. His closest allies, in fact, were Catholics, who suffered under the same constraints.

But as he walked through the city streets on some of the hottest days of summer, he wondered what Mitre Street would be like. And as he rode to Surrey and felt the country breeze blow away the dust and smells of London, he couldn't help but wonder if Miss Deborah Cohen ever had a day's relief from summer in the East End.

And so, a week or two into July, he found himself again in front of the Cohens. This time it was during business hours, and he introduced himself to the clerk and asked if Miss Cohen was available. The man scurried off to the rear, and in a few moments David was face-to-face not with Miss Cohen, but with an imposing, heavyset gentleman who identified himself as Jacob Cohen.

"And just who might you be, asking after my daughter?"

"I am Sir David Treves, Mr. Cohen. I met your daughter a few weeks ago when I escorted Mr. Goldsmid home."

"Oh, you're the fine gentleman Deborah told me about," replied Cohen, his face softening a little. "We were both grateful to you for your good deed. But I did not realize that you were an acquaintance of Deborah's."

"I cannot really claim acquaintance, Mr. Cohen," David said. It was a new experience for him to be evaluated by a protective father. "But I would like to get to know your daughter better. In fact, I was wondering if I might convince you to lend her to me for an afternoon's drive to Richmond."

"I may only be a small tradesman, Sir David, but I know what is due my daughter."

"Of course, she would bring her abigail."

"Of course, I have no abigail." The clerk, having done his duty to his master, had then informed the mistress of the home that she had a caller, and Deborah had just appeared behind her father.

"I am happy to see you again, Miss Cohen," said David, with a bow. "I was just asking your father's permission to take you out of the heat and dust of the city."

"Mr. Tre-ves is the gentleman I told you about, Father."

"Sir David, Deborah."

"A baronet?" she inquired coolly.

"Yes, the title went to me, although both Father and

Grandfather deserve it far more for their long service to their country."

"You have been working very hard, my dear," said Mr. Cohen. "I could spare you for one afternoon. But you would need a companion, nevertheless."

"I will ask Sarah to accompany me, Father."

Mr. Cohen's face brightened. "That would be splendid. And a rare treat for her as well as you."

"The day after tomorrow, then, Miss Cohen?"

"All right, Sir David." Her acceptance of his invitation was given in as indifferent a tone as a refusal might have been, and David wondered, as he made his way through the filthy streets, just why he had invited the little redheaded witch.

Two days later, as he lifted her up into his curricle, he wondered again. There was no sign of enthusiasm or welcome on her face, although this lack was more than made up for by her little companion. Treves had expected some older neighbor. Sarah turned out to be a scrawny, dark-haired little thing who looked to be about eight or nine. She chattered nonstop as they made their way slowly through the streets, but fell silent when they reached the highway.

"Are you all right, Sarah?" inquired David.

Sarah flushed. "I just never seen so much green before, sir."

"Sarah has never been out of the East End, Sir David."

"And you, Miss Cohen?"

"Not often. When my mother was alive, we would occasionally take a picnic to Hampstead Heath. But usually we were too busy to go anywhere."

When they reached Richmond, David helped both Deborah and Sarah down, while his groom spread rugs on the grass and opened the picnic baskets. As Sarah watched the china plates and linen napkins being set out, her eyes got wide. And when the silver was unwrapped, she gave a little jump and a squeal of delight. "She has never seen silver before?" asked David, after they began to eat.

Deborah seemed to be choking on a bread crumb and took a great swallow of lemonade. "Why, no, I am sure she has seen it, just not so much of it, perhaps."

"Does she work for you and your father, Miss Cohen?" asked David, after Sarah had finished eating and run off to play under Tompkins's watchful eye.

"Yes, we have started training her as a kitchen maid. She is our tenth," Deborah announced proudly.

"Your tenth maid? Surely you are not that difficult to work for," David teased.

"I can be very difficult, Sir David," replied Deborah, with a gleam in her eye.

"Of that I have no doubt, Miss Cohen. But not, I imagine, with eight-year-old kitchen maids."

"Sarah is almost twelve, Sir David."

"But she is so small."

"Not enough food and light does tend to stunt a child's growth, sir. What we have done over the past few years is try to give a few girls an alternative to the streets. I have managed to place all my maids in good houses."

"Was Sarah on the streets?"

"Not in the sense you mean, Sir David."

"She would have been a peddler of some sort, then?" he asked, relieved that such a young girl had escaped prostitution.

"You could say she was in trade," replied Deborah, with a smile that she quickly hid with her napkin.

"What you are doing is quite admirable, Miss Cohen."

"What I am doing is but a drop in the bucket," she replied with some bitterness. "But I try not to think of all the other girls out there and concentrate on the one I can help."

"Well, I didn't bring you out here to talk of the horrors of the East End. Come," said David, extending his hand, "let us take a stroll. Sarah will be quite safe with Tompkins."

"But will I be safe with you?"

"I assure you, I am not the sort to ravish respectable young women."

"Hmmm. Does that mean that you are the sort to ravish young women who are not respectable?"

David looked down at Deborah. She was trying to keep her face straight, but burst out laughing when he started to sputter a protest.

"That is the first smile you have given me, Miss Cohen. Although your humor is at my expense, I take it as a good sign."

"A good sign of what, Sir David?"

"Our future acquaintance."

"You intend to know me better?"

"I most certainly hope so, Miss Cohen."

"Why, Sir David? I most certainly would not fit in with any of your friends."

"Why not? First, don't be so sure that my friends wouldn't appreciate you."

"Second?"

"It is your red hair and matching temper that draws me, I must confess. I have never *seen* such hair," said David with exaggerated awe. "My family is all dark, like me."

Deborah blushed and walked faster so that she drew ahead of him on the path. Her hair, which was only loosely bound in back, was glorious in the sun, and her trim figure more than compensated for the plainness of her gown.

David caught up with her at the small duck pond where the path ended.

"Look at the cygnets," she whispered, pointing out an elegant swan and her two offspring. "We should have brought Sarah with us."

David had to stand very close to her to remain on the path, and he felt Deborah shiver.

"You are chilly, Miss Cohen?"

"No, no, not at all, Sir David."

"Do you suppose we could be more than acquaintances, Miss Cohen?"

"Do you mean friends?" asked Deborah softly, her eyes still on the swans.

"I most certainly hope so," David replied, turning her chin toward him with the tip of his finger.

Deborah blushed and chattered on about how they must get back to Sarah, who would be worried by now. She started out, and David made sure he was next to her as they walked, letting his hand brush hers, and supporting her under her arm when they came to barely perceptible puddles.

When they got back, Sarah and Tompkins had their heads bent over a pair of dice. Her lap was full of the silver, while he had only one spoon left.

"The little wench is a marvel, Sir David." Tompkins grinned. "You'd 'ave no silver left if you'd come along any later."

"Give the silver back, Sarah," said Deborah sternly.

" 'Twas only a game, my dear," said David.

"All of it, Sarah."

Sarah grimaced and pulled a small salt cellar out of her pocket.

"And anything else."

David was about to protest, but when he saw his watch dangling from Sarah's small hands and his silk pocket handkerchief, he closed his mouth with an almost audible snap.

"Tell Sir David what you did on the streets, Sarah," Deborah said.

"I lifted things."

"Lifted things?"

"Yes. 'andkerchiefs, purses, and the loike. I were wery good at it, too. Still am, ain't I, sir?" she added with a mischievous smile. "I were going to give it all back, Miss Deborah, honest I was. I just wanted to see if I 'ad lost my touch."

Tompkins, who had been standing there, his eyes open in astonishment, threw his head back and laughed. "Now don't that beat all, Sir David!"

"Yes, Tompkins, it does," David replied slowly and sternly. "You were supposed to be watching her, and not teaching an innocent child games of chance."

"Me teach 'er! It were 'er dice, sir," protested Tompkins as he picked up the rugs and picnic basket and dumped them unceremoniously into the carriage to protest the unfairness of it all. "Hinnocent indeed!"

David reconsidered. "I apologize, Tompkins. Hardly innocent, you are right. Into the carriage, ladies. And Sarah, your hands clasped in your lap all the way home, my girl."

"Yes, sir. Sorry sir."

"I am sure she meant to give them back, Sir David," murmured Deborah.

"That may be so, but I'll not take any chances."

Sarah, who had been studiously watching her fingers lace and unlace in her lap, peeked up at David's face and, satisfied there was more amusement than outrage there, relaxed. She would have hated to be responsible for scaring the 'ansome gentleman away from Miss Deborah.

16

The ride back was quiet, Sarah having dozed off after the first mile.

"Tired out from her criminal activities, no doubt," whispered David with a smile.

"It isn't funny, you know."

"I know. It is appalling to think of any child that proficient. I knew petty thievery is common, of course, but this is the first time I've seen a child who did it. Sarah is very lucky to be with you, Deborah. I admire you for your charity."

"And is this picnic one of your charitable deeds, Sir David?" Deborah hated being praised for something she did because it seemed the only thing to do, and so she was all prickles again. And she did not want to think that Sir David's interest might only be charitable.

"If by a charitable deed you mean one where one puts up with unpleasantness for the sake of congratulating oneself for the sacrifice, then perhaps it is, Miss Cohen. For you most certainly show a genius for unpleasantness," replied David, stung to anger. He had never met such a hedgehog of a woman, prickling up at the least kindness or easy compliment.

"I am sorry, Sir David. That was unfair of me," said Deborah with genuine feeling. "It has been a great treat to get out into the country. You have been every bit a gentleman, and I am acting most ungrateful."

"I don't want your gratitude, young woman," growled David.

"What do you want, then?"

"Your friendship."

"Why? I am sure you have a great many good friends, all of whom move in the first circles of society."

"I don't know," replied David honestly. "I do have good friends. In fact, there is one in particular whom I would love to introduce you to. I think you would like Lady Barbara. But none of my friends has such . . ."

"Red hair and the temperament that goes with it?"

"Not to mention freckles, Miss Cohen."

"Of course. My freckles. I should have known they were the attraction all along." Deborah sighed in mock despair.

"It is your mercurial nature, I think—your ability to blow hot and cold in almost the same instant—that keeps me interested. And seriously, Miss Cohen, I would like to take you out for another drive, if I may."

Deborah was silent for a few minutes. There was every reason to say no. Treves was way beyond her and only intrigued, no doubt, by that distance between them. And when that fascination wore off, what would be left? Yet she wanted to know him better and, she had to admit to herself, she wanted more brushing of arms and fingers on chins, and even lips on lips.

"Yes, yes, you may call again, Sir David."

When they reached Mitre Street, David dropped Deborah and Sarah off and made them promise to accompany him the next week. Just as his carriage was starting off, he heard someone call from behind him. It was Malachi, his basket full of oranges. David signaled the groom to stop, and the old man caught up to them.

"Be ye headed in my direction, Sir David?" asked Malachi, taking an orange and rubbing it on his sleeve and handing it up to his rescuer.

"Only in that we are leaving the East End," said David.

"But climb in, and we will drop you off as close as we can to the Drury Lane."

"Thankee, sir."

David grabbed the fruit basket and placed it on the seat next to him, and then extended his hand. Malachi plopped down and gave him a gap-toothed grin.

"I see ye be courting our Miss Deborah."

"Hardly courting, Mr. Goldsmid," said David in his most dignified tones. "It has been so warm that I just thought I would get Miss Cohen into the fresh air of Richmond."

"But I heard ye say that ye was coming again next week."

"A drive or two in the country is hardly courting," protested David.

"So ye say, so ye say. But she be a good woman, our Deborah. Took me in when times were hard. And a fine-looking woman, too." This last was accompanied by a wink so exaggerated that David could only laugh.

. "I am really not looking to get married yet, Mr. Goldsmid."

"Call me Malachi. And above all, she be a fine Jewish woman."

"And if I were," continued David, "whether the young woman were Jewish or not would hardly enter into it at all."

Malachi was genuinely shocked. "I am sorry to hear ye say so, Sir David. Oh, there's too many around here marrying any Betsy or Mary. But I would have thought that ye, being a fine gentleman, would want a woman of your own faith. For if their mother isn't Jewish, then your sons won't be."

"I know that, Malachi," said David. "But I confess to you that I do not care whether my wife is Jewish or Christian, so long as she has the qualities I am looking for."

"And what might they be, Sir David?"

"I am looking for a woman who is sweet and quiet, from

a good family. She need not be beautiful, but at least pretty."

"I used to be looking for someone like that before I wed Mrs. Goldsmid."

"You are married, Malachi?"

"Used to be. Rachel is dead. When it got too hard living alone, that's when I moved upstairs to the Cohens'."

David offered his sympathies.

"Oh, I still do miss her. But we had a great time before she was taken. Yes, I had my eye out for a dainty little miss like ye've been describing, but my Rachel, with her black hair and snapping black eyes fair took my breath away. I were just beginning to court little Rebeccah Schwartz when I met Rachel. I never looked at another woman for more than thirty-five years. But were I younger, I'd be looking at Miss Deborah. Except for her red hair, she fair reminds me of Rachel. She's got that same spirit."

"Ah, yes. Red-haired and spirited does describe Miss Cohen."

"Say what ye like, Sir David, but ye didn't come back to Mitre Street just to be charitable. Ye came back to see Miss Deborah again. Ye be used to those meek and mild society misses I see outside the opera. Washed-out little girls, they are. Our Miss Deborah, she is a real woman. Knows her own mind and lets ye know it too. Well, here is the theater. Ye can let me out here."

David helped the old man down, and climbed down himself to hand him his oranges.

"Thankee, Sir David. I'll be seeing ye again," said Malachi. "Ye remember what I said."

David watched the old man walk down the street, brushing off urchins who tried to steal an orange or two. He was amazed Malachi hadn't melted away, for he had his old black coat on, despite the heat. A character, Malachi Goldsmid, but a courageous one. It took courage to go back night after night and risk public abuse. It took spirit, thought David. The inhabitants of Mitre Street that he had met so far were admirably spirited. And Malachi was partly right. David might not be interested in courting her, but Deborah Cohen was the most interesting woman he had met in a long time and he fully intended to enjoy more of her company.

17

Arundel was only a few miles from the sea, and when she arrived, Barbara was delighted by the smell of saltwater. Her welcome left nothing to be desired. Wardour was obviously delighted to see her, greeting her with far less reserve than he usually showed, and introducing her proudly to the household staff who lined the drive.

"My mother is in the morning room and is eager to meet you, my dear," said Wardour as he led her up the steps.

"As I am to meet her." Actually, Barbara was more than eager. She imagined Lady Wardour to be tall, like her son, and a woman used to managing things, having been left with an estate to run and a son to raise on her own. And so, when they entered the morning room and saw only a sweet-faced little woman, Barbara assumed her to be Lady Wardour's companion. It was a complete surprise to realize that this diminutive lady was her future mother-in-law.

"I am delighted you are here, my dear," said Wardour's mother. "Peter has told me so much about you that I feel I know you already."

"I am happy to be here," replied Barbara. It was clear from the doting look she gave him as she mentioned his name that Peter was the apple of his mother's eye. It obviously would have been quite easy for her to have spoiled him. That the only sign of indulgence was his subtle air of taking for granted that all would naturally go his way said a great deal for his parent.

Barbara came to appreciate Lady Wardour more and

more. It was clear that although she doted on Peter, she had raised him to think of others, not only himself. Barbara had been impressed with his conversations about Arundel, but now that she was there, she saw the full extent of his involvement. He was up early every morning. After they breakfasted together, he was off to meet with his estate manager. He apologized in advance for his morning neglect of her, but made clear he was available in the afternoons. Barbara got into the habit of a long after-breakfast walk, coffee with Lady Wardour later in the morning, and then an introduction, each day, to the details of managing Arundel. Lady Wardour might look fragile, but she knew the household concerns as well as Wardour knew the estate. Barbara was eager to learn, for since Robin had married, Diana had been acting mistress of Ashurst. Barbara was very much looking forward to taking charge of her own household.

In the afternoons, she and Lady Wardour entertained neighbors or made visits themselves. And just before tea, she and Peter had lovely rides exploring the countryside and once or twice going for a wild gallop on the beach. After supper one of them would read aloud for a while, and every night Lady Wardour would make sure to excuse herself early enough so that Wardour and Barbara had some time together alone.

The first night she did so, Barbara turned to him, expecting him to share her amusement at his mother's little strategy. Instead, he apologized for her.

"I hope you don't think Mother is trying to place you in an uncomfortable situation. I am sure she feels it is acceptable to leave us alone since we are betrothed."

"Indeed, I am most grateful to her for her thoughtfulness," said Barbara, trying to tease him into a lighter mood.

"So am I, my dear," he replied. "I was just worried about what you might think."

Barbara breathed an inner sigh of relief at his words and moved closer to him on the sofa.

"I was hoping that we might continue becoming familiar

with one another's kisses," she said, surprised by her own boldness.

Wardour pulled her to him and began kissing her gently. Then his hand slipped around her shoulders and hers behind his head and they pulled each other closer. It was a long, deep, satisfying kiss, and Barbara wanted it to go on forever. Wardour ended it far too soon.

"We must watch ourselves, my dear. I am not one of those men who cannot wait for the wedding, although I must admit that I am tempted."

There was a longer kiss the next night. But the pattern was set. Barbara sensed passion in Wardour, but a passion always easily restrained. She supposed she should be grateful for his restraint, but she wasn't. She wanted to feel him let go, so that she could. So far there was affection, enjoyment of each other's company, and mutual attraction, all of the ingredients of love. But somehow the ingredients stayed separate. What was needed was the alchemy of unrestrained feeling, or so Barbara thought night after night. Rationally, she knew that all should combine after marriage, when Wardour would feel less constrained. But irrationally, she wanted to experience that final combining now, so that she would feel that love was there, not just know that the conditions were right for it.

18

Peter had shown a great deal of thoughtfulness in his preparations for her visit. The guest room Barbara occupied had been redecorated for her. She was introduced to their neighbors, and one day he escorted her to town so that she would become familiar with the shopkeepers who supplied the household. He also had had the old fortepiano, which had been under holland covers in the corner of the ballroom, dusted, polished, and tuned. It had been moved into the larger drawing room so that Barbara could play whenever she wished.

She had brought no music with her and would have ignored the instrument had Lady Wardour not revealed to her the trouble her son had gone to. Barbara felt an obligation to play a little, just to show her gratitude. So for a short time during the day she would practice pieces she knew by heart, and varied their evenings together occasionally by playing for Wardour and his mother. Both nodded during the music and clapped politely, but Barbara could tell that neither was a music lover. Given that fact, she was even more touched by Peter's thoughtfulness.

She was correct about her fiancé. He was not a devotee of the arts, but a down-to-earth practical man who tolerated others' interest in painting, theater, and music. He had been a bit worried when he had first met Barbara, for he had heard of her prodigious talent. He took it on faith, this talent, for even after he'd heard her play, the only judgment he felt equipped to make was that she played rather passionately and that she never misplayed a note. He was not tone-deaf, but listening to music for him was like listening to a foreign language. As his interest in Barbara grew, his only hesitation was about what it might be like married to a woman who spoke a language he could not comprehend.

He had been relieved, therefore, to see that Barbara's passion for music seemed to have diminished. He liked to think it was his courtship that had drawn her interest away from music and toward himself. He had taken it for granted, in fact, that being his wife and a mother to their children would be a more acceptable way of channeling her creative energy.

But since he didn't expect her to give up her music completely and since he prided himself on his understanding and generosity, he had the fortepiano prepared and encouraged her to play. And was duly relieved to see that she spent so little time with it.

A week or so into her visit, after his mother had taken herself off to bed and before they had become too distracted by the night's ration of kisses, Wardour commented on her lack of interest.

"I have noticed you have not spent much time at the piano, Barbara."

"Oh, I hope you don't think I don't appreciate your thoughtfulness, Peter. It is only that I had almost given up playing altogether this spring."

Wardour smiled. "It had seemed to me that you were giving it less time, my dear. In fact, I was rather gratified to think that I was such a distraction."

Wardour's smile held more than a hint of self-satisfaction, and for one moment Barbara was tempted to wipe it off his face with a slap. She was immediately horrified at her reaction. Her attention *had* been given to him during the spring and he had every right to assume a connection. It was only that at some very deep level he expected everything in his life would work out the way he, the Marquess of Wardour, wanted it to.

She wanted very much to say, "Do not assume so readily, Peter, that all lives revolve around your own," but that would have been too harsh. Instead, she explained that she had devoted many years to her music, only to finally realize that no amount of talent would change the fact that performance opportunity was limited due to her rank and sex. "Had you not so kindly prepared the piano for me, I would not have expected to play at all. I must say, though, Peter, that I do enjoy playing for you and your mother, so perhaps I can allow music a place in my life after all."

Wardour slipped an arm around her. "I have always thought music, drawing, and embroidery and such were very appropriate activities for young girls and women as respites from their domestic duties. I am happy to see music become less of a passion. I hope, Barbara, that another kind of passion will more than make up for it."

Barbara had no chance to reply, for Wardour's mouth covered hers demandingly. It was lucky for them both that his caresses were much less restrained than usual. Barbara felt his hand slip behind her neck and undo a tape or two on her gown so that he could stroke her back gently and then, reaching in front, cup one of her breasts in his hand. She was so distracted by these new pleasures he was introducing her to that she forgot her anger at his equating her music to something like embroidery.

19

The marquess and his mother had planned a dinner for Barbara's more formal introduction to the neighbors. They invited a small group of guests for a private concert of chamber music and then a light supper. After that, more of the neighbors were invited to enjoy dancing and light refreshments in the ballroom.

Although Lady Wardour had been most willing to let Barbara learn the ins and outs of the household, she refused to let her lift a finger for the festivities. "This is *your* party, my dear, so you should not have to work at all." After protesting, Barbara gave up and kept herself busy riding, walking, and practicing, for Wardour had specially requested that she play a tune.

The day before the dinner dance she was in the music room halfheartedly running through a Beethoven sonatina when the door opened and Wardour walked in.

"Excuse me, my dear, I didn't realize you were here, you were playing so softly. Come in, Mr. Gower, come in."

Barbara was amazed to see her wandering Scotsman follow her fiancé into the room. Before she could say anything, Peter introduced him as one of the musicians he had hired for the next week's party.

"I was assured by the vicar that he is an excellent musician and can scrape a fiddle for the dancing besides. I wanted you to meet him, and I am sure he will want to know what you intend to play. I thought you might enjoy a duet. Mr. Gower, my fiancée, Lady Barbara Stanley."

Gower bowed politely and Barbara nodded her head, still a bit dazed by his sudden arrival. And by his appearance. Gone was the long hair and beard. He was dressed in a very acceptable albeit worn pair of pantaloons and a forest-green jacket. Barbara could not help looking down at his legs, now encased in boots, and thought that in some ways a kilt was more attractive. How strange that I know Mr. Gower's legs better than Peter's, she thought.

Wardour excused himself and left them to become better acquainted.

"What on earth are you doing in Arundel, Mr. Gower? And looking like this?" demanded Barbara.

"Ah, ye dinna like me in trews, then, lassie? Ye prefer the kilt? I hae verra guid legs, if I do say so maself."

"You may look a bit more like a gentleman, but you are as outrageous as ever, Mr. Gower. How ever did my fiancé come to hire you?"

"I play for the local gentry as well as at fairs, Lady Barbara. I play wherever I will be paid for it. The vicar heard me playing a little Mozart one morning and asked me to play with him one evening. And then he recommended me to the marquess."

"But what are you doing here at all?"

"I am a traveling musician, lass. Therefore I travel!"

"Of course," said Barbara with some asperity.

"Have ye decided what we are to play, then, lass?"

"You cannot call me lass, Mr. Gower."

"No, you are quite right, Lady Barbara," Gower replied rather sadly. "Someone might comment on the familiarity."

"Exactly." Barbara was glad he was quick to understand, but a bit disappointed, for she rather liked being called lass. "There were to be several selections for cello and fortepiano, played by the vicar and his wife. And I was to play one piece, although I have not decided what."

Alec leaned over and looked at Barbara's music. "A sonatina. And some Bach? Aye, a typical evening's entertainment. I had thought you were more of a musician than that."

"As I think I once told you, I have not been playing much lately, Mr. Gower."

"And does that not bother you, Lady Barbara?"

"Not really, Mr. Gower," Barbara told him in a tone that forbade any further comment.

"Aye, it is none of my business, your face tells me. Well, now that you have a violin, what pieces do you have in mind?"

Barbara rifled through the sheets of music the vicar had sent over. "Here is a suitable trio. Lively enough to keep our guests awake."

"Wait a moment. Is that a Mozart sonata?" asked Alec, reaching over and placing his hand on Barbara's.

"Why, yes. The Sonata in B flat for fortepiano and violin. But we are to be four."

"Is there any objection to us playing a duet together? This is certainly a piece more appropriate to your skill than the sonatina."

"I suppose we could. But I have never played this before, and indeed, have not played many duets, but confined myself to solo music."

"No matter, lass. Excuse me, 'my lady.' Start exploring your part and I will be right back with my fiddle." Gower was gone before she could protest. Playing a short solo was one thing. But this duet would mean hours of practice, and she was not sure she wanted to throw herself back into music that way. But she opened the sheets and began running through her part. It *was* a lovely piece, she thought, and she forgot her surroundings and became lost in the music. She was able to follow the violin score after a few minutes, and began to hum it softly. She was so engrossed that she did not hear Gower's return, and when he started to play, it was as though the music in her head had magically materialized, so expert was his entry.

They both stumbled over a few measures, but their first

attempt convinced Barbara that it would be a rare treat to play with someone, especially one so talented.

"I should have guessed from your fiddle-playing that such skill would carry over into a different kind of music. I don't think I have ever met anyone as versatile before. I am not sure I can do you justice."

"The composer wrote this for both instruments, Lady Barbara, and you more than do it justice, ma dear," he replied, rolling his *r*'s. "But we do need more than a few hours' practice. Do you have the time?"

"I can meet you here in the late morning and perhaps a few afternoons. Lady Wardour has effectively taken over the preparations for the dance, but I would not like to neglect my fiancé. Where are you staying, Mr. Gower?"

"At the inn in Arundel, my lady."

"That is a walk. I can send the carriage for you."

"No, thank you, Lady Barbara. You forget, I am used to long walks. And late morning will be fine with me."

Barbara stood up and waited for him to place his violin in its battered old case. She extended her hand and said gratefully, "It will be a privilege to play with you, Mr. Gower."

Alec wanted to take her hand and bring it to his lips, but contented himself with a gentle squeeze. He reminded himself, as he walked back to the inn, that he was still only a busker, and Lady Barbara a very happily betrothed young woman.

20

For the next few days, Alec and Barbara shut themselves up in the music room, admitting no one except the vicar and his wife, who came to practice their trio. The Mozart piece was not technically difficult, but required a perfect blending of the two instruments. But the blending was subtle, and in some movements, it was the violin that the uneducated listener would hear and respond to. The violin needed the fortepiano, in the same way a bird's song needed the sound of a brook or the wind in the trees. The song would be diminished if heard alone, but your everyday listener would never realize that. "Listen to the lark," he or she would say.

Barbara didn't really mind that the audience might appreciate Gower's part more. He and she knew that it took great talent to allow the violin to sing without either competing with it or disappearing altogether. And there were moments of such sweetness that Barbara could only marvel that someone as large as Gower could produce them. His may be a natural talent, thought Barbara one morning as they sat silent a minute after bringing the piece to a close, but he must have had some formal training.

She turned to Alec, who gave her a smile as sweet as their music. It affected her as much as one of Wardour's kisses. But she should not be thinking of kisses. . . .

"Mr. Gower, you play so well that I cannot believe you have not studied somewhere. In fact, you remind me of one of your countrymen."

"Oh, aye, lass, and who would ye be thinking of?"

"Of Robert Burns, of course. The man with two voices—that of a Scots plowman, and the other, an educated gentleman. And your music is like your accents: you can slip from one to the other. Surely you are not just an uneducated wanderer?"

"And what if I were, lass? 'A man's a man for a' that.'"

"Of course. I did not mean to insult you, Mr. Gower. Merely to point out that I think you disguise the fact that you have had some education."

"I am found out, Lady Barbara," said Alec with an exaggerated bow. "You are right, I have had some classical training."

"Then why do you wander around playing fairs and busking? You could find employment in London, I am sure."

"Weel, I enjoy the outdoors, and prefer the country in good weather. I expect I will head to town when it gets cold. That answers your second question. As to the first, my family had means enough to educate me, but would have preferred me to be anything but a musician."

Barbara imagined Gower as the son of a wealthy farmer or tradesman, who of course would not approve of a dilettante in the family.

"What would they have preferred? That you enter the family business?" Barbara knew she was prying, but was too intrigued to resist.

"In a manner of speaking, yes."

"And so you chose a vagabond life instead of a settled one. Has it been worth it?"

Alec thought of the nights he had been without food or shelter. There hadn't been many, but all of them seemed to have occurred in bad weather. He remembered his first month on the road, and how disorienting and painful it had been to be treated with no respect and sometimes hostility. Not everyone considered a busker a "traveling musician." Many regarded him as a beggar and treated him as one. But then there were the days when the music seemed to flow through him and it didn't matter that he was in a small town on market day instead of in front of an educated audience. And there was the freedom of the open road before him, the satisfaction of finding a good pace and reaching his destination tired, but satisfied by his physical exertion. And rewarded by a tankard of frothing ale. No champagne had ever come close to homebrewed, in his opinion. And there was Barbara herself.

"Aye, it has been worth it, my lady. Not least of all because I have met you."

Barbara blushed and didn't know what to say. There was a sort of friendship that had grown between them because of their practice, but surely he didn't mean anything else?

"I have never before had the opportunity to play with such a fine musician," Alec continued.

Barbara was relieved. He had only been talking about the sympathy between them as they played and not anything more. She had been frightened for a moment. But there was nothing else, she quickly told herself. How could there be? She was happily betrothed to a man of her own rank.

She folded the music closed and rose from the piano. "I think we are ready for our first public appearance, Mr. Gower. Perhaps we should plan on a few minutes with the vicar and his wife just before tomorrow's concert."

"I will be here early, Lady Barbara."

"Good day, then, and thank you for both your confidences and compliments." Barbara left without looking back and Alec watched her go. He wondered where her blush came from. Had she guessed he meant more than just a musical compliment? "Ah, weel," he muttered out loud as he picked up his instrument, "and what would a fine lady like herself want with a great gawk like me?"

Alec looked nothing like a great gawk the next evening. He had managed to buy himself a new shirt, and had charmed the innkeeper's wife into brushing and pressing

his knee breeches and evening coat. He might not look like
a fine gentleman, with his worn cuffs, but at least he was
presentable.

A bit more than presentable, all the ladies would have
agreed as they admired the way his black evening clothes
set off his blue eyes. He looked like a gentleman, standing
there next to the vicar and Lady Barbara, and it was easy to
forget he was only a hired musician.

The guests sat quietly and clapped politely after the trios.
But when the vicar and his wife stepped down and joined
the audience, leaving Barbara to join Alec, the opening bars
of the sonata demanded more than polite attention. A few
people, like the vicar and his wife, realized that the caliber
of the performance was equal to any on a concert stage.
The others only knew that this duet was as enjoyable a
piece as they had ever heard.

Lady Wardour looked over at her son during the performance. He seemed more concentrated than usual, but that
was understandable, since it was his fiancée playing. She
wondered, given his lack of genuine interest in music, if he
could really appreciate Barbara's talent. It was a revelation
to her that this charming young woman who had spent so
much of her time assiduously learning all about the household, was transformed when she played into a brilliant and
powerful performer. She turned her attention to Gower,
whose auburn hair glinted in the light as he bent his head
over his violin. Now there was a comparable talent, she
thought, and what a wonderful partnership they had
formed. She realized that she had picked up on a sympathy
between them as musicians that was almost palpable, and
found herself wondering if such a sympathy existed between her son and Barbara. Of course, there must be, she
reassured herself. And will be, as they begin to produce a
family.

The applause was spontaneous and unrestrained, and
Barbara and Alec flushed with pleasure as they took their
bows.

"Encore!" someone cried enthusiastically.

Wardour stood up and quieted the applause by holding up his hand. "I am sure that Lady Barbara and Mr. Gower would love to oblige you, but supper, alas, awaits us." He was every inch the perfect host, thoughtful of guests and performers alike, moving them into the dining room. It was quite reasonable not to allow another piece, thought Alec as he followed the vicar toward the dining room. But I wonder if he also doesn't want the future marchioness so much the center of attention for musical performance.

Barbara had gone into the dining room first, having been escorted by the vicar. She always experienced a letdown after playing, as though having been lifted up by a wave of music, she was now experiencing the ebb. She barely heard what Wardour was saying and had left all seating arrangements to Lady Wardour, so she didn't notice until she was seated that Mr. Gower was nowhere to be seen.

In fact, Alec had been rudely jolted out of his own post-performance letdown. He had been next to the vicar's wife, congratulating her on her own skill, when suddenly the marquess was in front of him.

"Mr. Gower, we have arranged a light supper for you belowstairs," Wardour said politely. "If you will follow James here," he continued, motioning to one of the footmen, "he will take you down. A wonderful performance, wonderful." Wardour patted him on the shoulder and then made his way into the dining room. The vicar's wife looked pained, and reaching out to Alec, shook his hand, saying, "It was a great privilege to play with you, Mr. Gower," before she followed her host into the dining room.

Alec was furious. That he, Alexander MacLeod, should be condescended to like that, was unimaginable. He wanted to pick Wardour up by his oh so well-arranged cravat and shake him. When the footman touched him on the arm and said, "This way, Mr. Gower," he almost turned on his heel and walked out the front door. But he controlled himself and followed the man downstairs. There was a tempting plate set out for him and a glass of cider, and he realized that he was indeed hungry and thirsty and had better eat or he would never be able to play afterward. As his anger drained away, he had to admit that there was no real reason to be so furious with Wardour. After all, no hired musicians sat as guests at his grandfather's table. Why he had expected to be treated differently, he wasn't sure. Perhaps it was because he had played with Lady Barbara as an equal and had therefore felt like one.

As soon as Barbara realized that Gower was not seated at the table and there was no empty place waiting for him, she turned to Wardour, who was seated on her right.

"Peter, I do not see Mr. Gower."

"Why, no, of course not, my dear. It would not at all be the thing to seat an employee at table with us. He is downstairs, where I promise you he is being fed well."

Barbara opened her mouth and then closed it. What was there to say? Wardour was right and she was not sure why she had expected Mr. Gower to be at supper. It would, in fact, have looked odd, as she thought of it from the marquess's perspective. But he had been an equal partner in the duet and somehow it felt wrong to exclude him. She was annoyed with Wardour and quite unjustly. His decision was an unexceptional one. What annoyed her, she decided, was that he was so complacent about it.

21

If Mr. Gower's exile to belowstairs bothered him, you could not tell from his playing, thought Barbara later in the evening as she danced a country dance with her fiancé. All the musicians were good, but it was Gower she listened for as she danced and as she socialized with her future neighbors. His versatility again struck her: she had heard him at a country fair, been amazed at his classical skill, and now heard him adapt to gentler dance music.

As the featured guest, she was in great demand and hardly sat down all evening. Her dances with Wardour were even more welcome than during the Season. Now that they had progressed to a greater physical intimacy, the touch of his hand around her waist during a waltz was more exciting than it had been in the spring. And he was clearly pleased with the evening. All his neighbors and friends had expressed their approval of his betrothed.

And why should they not? he thought to himself. She looked beautiful in her blue silk. The shade matched her eyes and the simple gold necklace set with small sapphires made one glance up and admire her hair. They were an attractive couple, he thought, not for the first time, and he smiled down at her.

"Are you happy, Barbara?"

Barbara, who had been lost in the music and the pleasant feelings his closeness brought her, looked up in surprise.

"Of course, Peter. Do you doubt it?"

"No, not really. I think I am feeling so satisfied with myself and my future bride that I just had to talk about it!"

"I am very happy, Peter," repeated Barbara, allowing him to pull her a little closer and ignoring the small voice inside her, which asked, "But if I am so happy, then why do I only feel that bubble of joy when I am with Alec Gower?"

Alec was apparently bent over his bow all evening, but Barbara was never far from his sight. She is magnificent, he thought, as he watched her dance. Tall and graceful and slender, with alluring curves revealed as the silk clung to her as she danced. She reminded him of the statues of goddesses he had seen in Greece.

There would be no dancing for him tonight. This was no Midsummer Fair, with all rules suspended. The fiddler ate belowstairs and most certainly could not approach a lady for a waltz. And after tonight, who knew when he would see her again, if ever? If he won his wager, and it certainly appeared he would, he'd move to London, but their paths were not likely to cross. From what he had heard, Wardour was very much a stay-at-home. Alec felt a great sadness at the thought of never again experiencing the joy of playing with Barbara. There had been more than a perfect blending of piano and violin. It had seemed like a very blending of souls. For his music came from his deepest self, and so, he thought, did hers.

Barbara was exhausted by the end of the evening. She had had to perform, act as hostess, and maintain polite conversation with people she barely knew. As soon as her guests had gone, she said her good-nights to Wardour and his mother and sought the solitude of her bedroom. She dismissed her maid as soon as her dress was over her head and slipped into her lawn nightrail. Just as she was about to slide under the covers, however, she heard it . . . the sound of a violin. It could only be Gower, she thought, and curious, she slipped on a dressing gown and crept down the stairs. The ballroom was dark except for one branch of candles by the musicians' platform. There was Gower, playing the loveliest, saddest piece Barbara had ever heard. He was playing softly, which only added to the feeling of lingering sadness.

She stood there and listened until the last note had died away. When Alec finally looked up, he saw her standing there and immediately stood up.

"Lady Barbara! Is there anything wrong? Can I help you?" he stammered.

"I heard the music and came down to listen. I thought you had already gone."

"I had a few drams with the other musicians, lass, and decided to wait a bit till my head cleared before I walked back to the inn."

"I thought strong liquor lifted one's spirits. The tune you were playing was very sad."

"Aye, I call it 'MacLeod's Lament.' "

"You wrote it? You are a composer also?"

"Almost all Scottish fiddlers can improvise and invent their own tunes, lass. Where do you think all the strathspeys and reels come from?"

"I confess I have never given it much thought, Mr. Gower. I have taken it for granted as something that is just there."

"Aye. The *real* composers are Mozart and Bach," replied Alec with a tinge of bitterness. "We keep our music as separate as we do the classes, don't we?"

"I suppose we do," Barbara said thoughtfully. "But that was as haunting a piece as any I've played or heard. I am privileged to have heard you play it."

"Thank you, my lady. And I am glad you were my audience of one." Although you could not have heard what the music was saying and be standing there in your nightclothes so coolly, he thought. For what was I lamenting but the fact I shall never have the right to kiss you or take you in my arms. "It is late, and you will get a chill standing here," said Alec. And if you don't get yourself off to bed, I will not answer for myself, he wanted to add.

Barbara had completely forgotten her state of undress and nervously pulled at her dressing gown. "Oh, yes, I must. Good night, Mr. Gower."

"Good-bye, Lady Barbara."

Barbara turned to go, and then stopped.

"Mr. Gower."

"Yes, Lady Barbara?"

"Will your travels take you to London?"

"Aye, as it gets colder I seek more indoor employment," he replied with a smile.

"Well, then, if you are in London this fall, you must look up a friend of mine. He is something of a patron of the arts and may be able to help you make your way in the city. His name is Sir David Treves."

"Why, that is kind of you, lass, to be thoughtful of me. I will look him up."

"Well, good night again." As she hurried back to her room, Barbara wondered just why she had given him David's name. Was it truly an unselfish suggestion to help him get the attention his talent deserved, or did she want to make sure she had some way of hearing about him?

22

David had invited Deborah and Sarah out for several drives during the summer. They revisited Richmond for another picnic and, at Sarah's request, rode one afternoon in Hyde Park. She had been eager to see where the quality went. David warned her that the park would be fairly empty during the summer, but as long as she saw a few lords and ladies, Sarah said she would be perfectly happy. Luckily for her, there were a few people out and David took great pleasure in pointing out a viscount and a duchess, and watching her eyes open wide.

"Now, Sarah," he teased, "surely you have lifted a handkerchief from an earl's pocket or cut the reticule from a lady's arm in the past?"

"I may 'ave, Sir David," she replied seriously, "but I never *knew* it were an earl or a duchess."

David couldn't help laughing, and when Sarah looked hurt, he assured her he wasn't laughing at her.

"You are quite at home here, Sir David," commented Deborah, having watched him lift his hand to acknowledge several greetings.

"You are surprised, Miss Cohen?"

"It is hard for me to comprehend such acceptance."

"One is not accepted everywhere. But yes, it is possible for a Jew to live the life of a gentleman."

"Does it not feel strange at times? Or rather, don't you feel like the stranger, Sir David?" Deborah's voice had lost its edge, and David could hear both curiosity and concern in it.

"There are certain places where I feel I am only tolerated because of my wealth, but I am certain by the time my children are grown, they will move freely in English society."

"And leave Judaism behind?"

"There are many Sephardim who are religious, Miss Cohen. I am not one of them, so I will have little to leave behind. And you and your father?"

"We do not attend temple regularly, nor keep to all dietary regulations," Deborah admitted. "But we observe the high holy days and the Sabbath. And I will always consider myself first a Jewish woman, then an Englishwoman. And although there are many intermarriages in the East End, I would never marry a Christian."

"Have you ever met a Christian, Miss Cohen?" David asked half humorously, half seriously.

"Of course, Sir David," Deborah replied tartly. "We do business with many of them."

"I meant socially."

"No, and I have never had the desire to."

"Hmmm. Well, perhaps I will have to remedy that," said David thoughtfully.

And so their next outing was to a small cottage on the edge of Hampstead. When Lord and Lady Vane had to be in town during the summer, they stayed on the Heath rather than in their town house, so they could pretend they hadn't left the country.

"Sarah," David announced as they drove through the village, "we will be meeting a viscountess."

Sarah's sat absolutely still. "You are not funning me, Sir David?"

"Certainly not." replied David, his eyes twinkling. But when they reached the cottage and were greeted by a small auburn-haired woman in an old muslin gown, Sarah pulled David aside as Nora introduced herself to Deborah.

"You lied to me," she said angrily.

"Of course I didn't."

"She can't be a viscountess. Look at 'er clothes," said Sarah disgustedly.

"David, introduce me to your other friend," said Nora, approaching them.

"This is Sarah, Miss Cohen's 'abigail' for the day, Lady Vane."

"I am pleased to meet you, Sarah."

"Now you got 'er in on it," muttered Sarah.

"In on what, David?" asked Nora.

"Sarah cannot believe you are a viscountess, Lady Vane."

Nora laughed and looked down at her dress. "I know I don't look much like one, Sarah, but I assure you David is telling the truth. My husband and I much prefer to be informal, which is why we enjoy our cottage retreat."

"Now, Sarah, curtsy to Lady Vane," said Deborah sternly.

"No, no," Nora protested as Sarah sank down to her knees.

"Don't worry, Lady Vane," said Deborah as Nora led them to a small table and chairs placed under the old apple tree, "Sarah has always dreamed of meeting quality. She will get great attention from the story of her curtsy on Mitre Street."

"Ah, yes, David told me you lived in the East End."

"My father is a wholesaler of fruit," announced Deborah with a glint in her eye.

"And David says you are his valued assistant and keep the books."

"I have always had a good head for figures, Lady Vane."

"I admire you, then, Deborah. My least favorite task before I was married was dealing with my publisher on financial matters. Now, come sit down, and help yourself to biscuits and lemonade. Sarah, there is an old swing over there that you might enjoy. It was my daughter's."

Sarah grabbed a few biscuits and sat herself down on the

swing. She let it move on its own, back and forth, back and forth, before she experimented with pushing off with her feet.

"That's right, Sarah," encouraged Deborah, "push and then lift your feet up."

Sarah slowly got the rhythm and Deborah turned to Nora and said, "I am afraid we'll never get her to leave. She has never been on a swing before."

"How sad," Nora commented.

"She never did have much chance to be a child, Lady Vane. She was out on the streets by the time she was seven."

"Yes, I forget how hard it is to be poor in the city. I am glad Miranda and I stayed in Hampstead when we first came south. At least there was fresh air and little crime. But let us forget depressing topics for a few moments, and enjoy the afternoon."

Nora skillfully got Deborah to reveal more of herself in a half hour than David had done in all their afternoons put together. He heard how her grandfather had come from Poland and in only a few years had moved from being a hawker to owning an outdoor stall. Deborah's father had been the one to expand the business to its present size.

"And what will happen when your father dies?" inquired Nora.

"I suppose that my husband-to-be will take it over."

"You are betrothed, then, Miss Cohen?" asked Nora.

David found himself holding his breath as he awaited her answer.

"Oh, no," said Deborah, blushing. "I just meant that one day I will no doubt marry someone who wishes to continue in the business."

Nora chatted on with Deborah for a few minutes and then turned to David.

"Excuse me, Miss Cohen, but I wished to share some news of a mutual friend with David," she said apologetically. "I received a letter from Lady Barbara yesterday, David."

David's face lit up and Deborah felt as though she were on the swing with Sarah and had pumped herself almost over the top before plunging back down to the ground. Of course Sir David had lady friends. Or, more to the point, friends who were ladies. She hadn't thought she believed his interest in her was more than curiosity at best or an attempt at eventual seduction at worst, but apparently she was as foolish as the next woman, for why else would she feel so awful at the thought of him with an English gentlewoman?

"She wrote from Arundel," Nora continued, "where she has met her prospective mama in-law, and appears to be quite happily getting to know Wardour's home."

Deborah's heart lifted as the full meaning of Nora's words sank in. Lady Barbara was only a friend. Of course, that still does not mean his interest in me is anything serious, she cautioned herself, but for the moment she was too relieved to heed her own warnings.

"How did you enjoy your visit, Miss Cohen?" David asked as they drove back to the city.

"Very much, thank you. Lady Vane is a lovely woman."

"I thought you would like her. She supported herself for years by her writing."

"So I gathered."

"That's why I thought you might be sympathetic to one another. You are both very much self-sufficient women."

"Do you see that as an admirable quality, Sir David?"

"Oh, yes."

"Then you are quite unusual, I think."

"Of course, independence need not preclude a close relationship with someone of the opposite sex."

"I do not see why it should," conceded Deborah.

"I am glad to hear that, Miss Cohen," David replied.

Deborah wondered if there was a deeper meaning to this
exchange and spent the next few days after their outing
alternating between hope, despair, and ironic self-castiga-
tion for her own foolishness.

23

David's calls to the East End had not gone unnoticed, and one day, over afternoon sherry, his father remarked upon his now regular absences.

"I assume it is a woman, David?"

"Why, yes, Father," replied his son coolly.

"It cannot be anyone your mother and I know, or surely you would have mentioned her name."

"No, you are right, it is no one you know."

"It is, of course, quite natural to have a mistress. But we were hoping, your mother and I, that you would soon be thinking of settling down and raising a family."

"Miss Cohen is not my mistress, Father." Yet, he added to himself. He certainly could not deny that he wanted her more each time he saw her. But she was a respectable woman, was Deborah Cohen, and he did not know if he had any chance of persuading her to a kiss, much less a liaison.

"Miss Cohen?" said his father.

"Miss Deborah Cohen. She is the daughter of a wholesaler in the East End."

"You are surely not considering anything serious with her, are you, David? We have not worked all these years to achieve a place in society only to have it thrown away. I was hoping, in fact, that you found Lord Sedgewick's daughter attractive."

"Yes, I know," David replied through gritted teeth.

"Marriage to a Christian woman would guarantee your children's future, David."

"It is not so much Lady Emily I find unattractive as her family. Her father is both a drinker and a gambler, and her mother is well-known for her indiscriminate choice of lovers."

"Ah, but the title is an old one. Our money for their title—a common enough bargain and you know it. But the Duke of Andlem has also made overtures to me, so it need not be Lady Emily if you don't like her. She is a bit young and spotty, I admit."

David had long been aware of his father's plans for him and had never questioned them. After all, the more secure a position in society he achieved, the better he would be able to effect political reform. But for some reason, today the thought of marrying some destitute nobleman's daughter galled him.

"I assure you, Father, I have not forgotten my obligations. Miss Cohen is someone I met by chance. I enjoy her company, and I like being able to do her the favor of getting her out of Mitre Street occasionally."

"No need to become agitated, my boy. I am sure you know what you are doing."

Actually, David was not at all sure he knew what he was doing. He had told part of the truth: he did enjoy Deborah's company and he did like to think he was making her life a little more enjoyable. But the more he saw her, the more he wanted to touch her, and the more frustrated he was with Sarah's presence. He didn't think he had a snowball's chance in hell of making her his mistress, but surely a kiss or two should not be impossible to bring about.

Accordingly, on his next visit he brought his niece's governess with him.

"This is Miss Crewe, Sarah. We are going to Kew Gardens today, and she has brought all kinds of sketching materials and will give you a lesson in botanical drawing." David tried to be matter-of-fact with his announcement, but the sharp look Deborah gave him made him feel obvious.

Sarah, however, was delighted. She had never had paper or paint available to her, and so she skipped happily along, looking for some "botanicals" to draw.

David let them get far ahead and guided Deborah to a bench in a secluded corner of the herb garden. It was a warm and sunny afternoon and the steady hum of bees and the faint scent of mint combined to relax Deborah's guard.

David looked down at her ink-stained hands, which rested quietly in her lap. He lifted one gently and brought it up for closer inspection.

"You have clerk's hands, Miss Cohen," he teased.

"As well I should, Sir David, keeping the ledgers as I do."

David bent down and kissed her fingers. Deborah started to pull away and protest, but David leaned down before she could utter a word and covered her lips with his.

To her shame, her protest died in her throat. The warmth of the sun, the bees, the spicy smell of the garden, had all combined to relax her, and the kiss undid her resolve. She had been wanting him to touch her for weeks. Not that she wanted to want him. But she did, beyond all reason.

David pulled back and smiled at the sight of her, eyes closed, face upturned.

"Do you always enjoy kissing that much, Miss Cohen?"

Deborah's eyes opened and she blushed a deep red. "No . . . I haven't done much kissing," she whispered. "But yes. I seem to enjoy it."

"We will have to remedy your lack of experience, then," said David, and pulled her closer.

Deborah wanted the next kiss to last forever, but David pulled away again.

"Don't," she whispered.

"Don't what?"

"Don't . . . stop."

David smiled down at her red head bent down in embarrassment at her own desire, and gently stroked the nape of her neck. Deborah felt small shivers go through her whole body.

"I have been wanting to kiss you for a long time, Miss Cohen. And now that I have, I want to go on kissing you. But I don't think I should."

"I know."

"What do you know?"

"I know what you want."

"I don't know how you could, when *I* don't. One thing I do know: I cannot take advantage of you," he said with a groan.

"I wish you could," replied Deborah, lifting her head.

"Do you?"

"No, not really," she said, some of her old spirit in her voice. "A part of me would like to be your mistress, Sir David, but I am too much the good accounting clerk to allow myself. I can see the debits and credits, and believe me, it would be me who ended up bankrupt," she added bitterly.

"You are correct. A respectable woman like yourself needs a husband, not a protector, however loving."

"I don't need your protection, thank you," said Deborah, moving away from him so she would not be tempted to give in and pull him down into another kiss.

"What shall we do, then, Miss Cohen? I very much enjoy your company. I have felt we could be friends, if nothing else."

"I have enjoyed these afternoons too, Sir David. But everything has changed, and I don't know if I should continue to see you."

"Well, I most certainly can't bring Miss Crewe again. Sarah can go back to being your chaperon, should you come out with me again. I promise we will not be too private."

"Let me think about it, please."

"All right, Miss Cohen. I do care about you, you know."

But not in the way I am beginning to care bout you, she thought as they rose to meet Sarah, who was running across the grass with her drawings in her hand.

24

Barbara spent a few more days at Arundel before returning to Ashurst for what was left of the summer. They were quiet days, spent with Wardour and his mother, with a short visit to the vicar breaking the pleasant monotony. She found it hard to leave, for she had begun to feel at home and wished she were safely married already. Why it felt unsafe to be unmarried wasn't a matter she wished to explore at any length.

The morning she left, she and Lady Wardour had tears in their eyes, and when Peter bade her good-bye, she clung to him in a manner most unlike her.

"What is it, my dear?" he asked.

"I just wish you could come with me and we would just continue on to Gretna," she answered.

Wardour smiled. "There is nothing I would like better, Barbara, but you know it is impossible. Come, cheer up! We will be wed in less than three months."

"I know I am being foolish. But it has been such a lovely visit and I am finding it hard to leave, now that I have come to know my new home."

"I am sorry that leaving makes you sad, but it is just what I hoped would happen if you visited, that you would come to feel Arundel was home. Now, in you go."

Barbara leaned out the window and waved until they were out of sight. She was very eager to be settled, to be mistress of Arundel and to be Wardour's wife and experience more than his kisses.

She didn't want to be returning to Ashurst, much as she loved it. She didn't want to be traveling north, for traveling in that direction reminded her of Mr. Gower, whom she needed to forget.

When she arrived home, she noticed that all the servants seemed subdued. It wasn't that they weren't happy to see her, but kept looking to the right and left of her, as though avoiding her face. She washed and changed quickly and went downstairs to look for her brother.

Barbara found both Robin and Diana sitting quietly next to one another on the sofa in the library. Robin was absent-mindedly stroking Diana's hair, and both looked more serious than Barbara had ever seen them.

"Is there something wrong, Robin? Not . . . not one of the children?"

"No, the twins are fine, Barbara," her brother assured her. "Come sit down."

"Then what is it? Something is very wrong, I can feel it."

"We just received word yesterday from Sutton . . ."

"Judith? The baby?"

"According to the letter, the baby came early . . . it was a difficult delivery . . . and . . ."

"And Simon is in danger of losing both of them." Diana finished what Robin couldn't.

"Why, she was not due for another month," protested Barbara, as though there were someone somewhere she could complain to rationally. She got up immediately. "I must go to her."

"We were only waiting for you to arrive, my dear," said Robin. "The carriage is ready."

All Barbara could think about as they drove to Sutton was her first days at school. She had been tall and gangly and shy. It had seemed that all the girls stared and giggled and whispered except for one small freckle-faced young woman who approached her and helped her find her room, and her place at table, and who cheered her up by saying, "Don't mind them. They'll stop staring by the end of the week and become friends. They're like this every time someone new arrives."

But Barbara already knew that she didn't want one of those vapid daughters of the *ton* for a friend. She had found her friend in Judith Ware. And had kept her over the years, despite distance and difference in rank. She felt ashamed of her recent anger at Judith, and her jealousy, and had the irrational sense that it was her resentment that had somehow caused this tragedy.

What would life be like without Judith to confide in? She hadn't confided much of her recent feelings, it was true, but she had been looking forward to a comfortable visit after the baby was born, when she could share both her happiness with Peter and her confused feelings about Alec Gower. To whom else could she ever admit her attraction to a wandering musician?

By the time they reached Sutton it was late afternoon. Barbara was terrified. What if the door opened and the butler was wearing a black armband? Please, God, please, spare my dear friend, she said over and over to herself as they walked up the front steps.

But the butler was not wearing black, and his face was creased in a smile that went from ear to ear. He ushered them into the drawing room, where Francis, the duke's secretary, was waiting.

"Cranston was smiling. He is either gone mad with grief—or is there good news?" asked Robin.

"Good news," said Francis quietly. "But it has been thirty-six hours of hell here, I assure you."

"What went wrong, Francis?" inquired Diana.

"Judith slipped going down the stairs out to the garden and her fall evidently brought on a premature labor. The baby was born five hours later. He was very tiny and weak, and she was hemorrhaging terribly. The doctor thought we might lose both of them."

"He, Francis? Then it was a boy. Judith was so sure. How is she dealing with the loss?" asked Barbara.

Francis rubbed his hand over his eyes and looked at her, puzzled. "Loss?"

"You said the baby was very tiny . . ."

"Oh, yes, and he still is small and weak, Lady Barbara, but the doctor managed to save both of them."

"Oh, thank God," said Barbara, tears of joy and relief streaming down her face. "Where is Simon? Can I see Judith?"

"The duke is in the nursery with Lady Sophy. You may go up, if you wish. Her grace is sleeping right now, but perhaps this evening . . . "

Barbara took the stairs two at a time, feeling as if she could fly. The door to the nursery was open halfway and she could hear Sophy humming quietly to herself. As she slipped in, Sophy looked up and raised her finger to her lips.

"My papa is very tired, Auntie Barbara. We mustn't wake him."

Simon was stretched out on the window seat, sound asleep. His clothes looked as if they hadn't been changed in a week, and his face was rough with stubble. It was only then, as she looked at him, that Barbara was able to imagine what the loss of Judith would have meant to him.

"My mama is sleeping too, and my new baby brother." Sophy's lower lip trembled.

Barbara opened her arms. "And here you are all alone, entertaining yourself, you brave girl. Come, sit on my lap and give me a hug."

Sophy crept onto Barbara's lap and clung to her. Barbara kissed the top of her head and felt the little girl's shoulders begin to shake.

"There, there, everything is all right now."

"But it wasn't for a long and scary time, Aunt Barb. And I'm afraid my mama has gone away after all."

"No, no, she really is just sleeping. Haven't you seen her?"

"No one would let me, Aunt Barb."

"No, I suppose not. I'll tell you what. Let us go down to the kitchen and get cook to make us some chocolate. Then, when you feel better, we'll tiptoe up to your mama's room and you can give her a kiss."

"Oh, thank you, Aunt Barb." Sophy gave her a hug. "Should we leave Papa here alone?"

"I think he needs the rest, Sophy. And he can find his way down when he wakes up."

"Yes, and it won't matter to Papa if he wakes up in the middle of the night," Sophy said proudly. "He can make his way in the dark better than anybody."

Barbara smiled down at the curly red head. How easily his daughter had accepted Simon's blindness as just another thing to know about him.

"Come, let's go before we wake him up."

The cook fixed them some cocoa and triangles of bread and butter. Sophy informed Barbara that when she ate in the nursery or the kitchen she was allowed to dip her bread into her chocolate. "It tastes better that way, Aunt Barb."

Barbara joined her in dipping and watched bread crumbs and butter swirl in her chocolate. The little circle of grease reminded her of her own childhood, when she and Robin had surreptitiously dipped their bread or toast into their cups.

Sophy started rubbing her hand over her eyes, and Barbara realized that the little girl was likely as exhausted as her father.

"Come, let us tiptoe up to Mama's room and blow her a kiss good-night."

There were candles still lit in Judith's room, and the housekeeper sat next to her bed. She looked up as they approached and motioned them in.

"You may come in, Lady Sophy, if you are as quiet as a little mouse," she said. Sophy tiptoed up to the bed, and Barbara could feel her hand trembling with the effort to hold herself back. She was sure the little girl wanted nothing more than to crawl into her mother's arms, and she was proud of her goddaughter's heroic efforts to behave like a grown-up.

Judith lay there, her cinnamon hair spread across the pillows, and her chest barely moving. Barbara looked in alarm at the housekeeper.

"Yes, she is exhausted, poor woman. But sleep is what she needs."

"I will lift you up, Sophy," whispered Barbara, "and you can kiss her good night."

Sophy gave Judith a kiss on the forehead and then turned and buried her face in Barbara's shoulder and started to sob. "I want my mama, I want my mama."

Barbara carried her out to the doorway.

"Now, now, Sophy, let me bring you up to bed and I will stay until you fall asleep. Then I will go down and sit by your mama, so the first thing she hears about when she wakes will be what a brave girl you are."

"She *is* going to wake up, isn't she?" asked Sophy, after Barbara had tucked her into bed.

"Oh, yes, darling." Barbara rhythmically rubbed her hand in a circle on Sophy's back until the little girl's breathing had become the even, steady breathing of sleep. Then she returned to Judith's room and whispered to the housekeeper that she would sit up for the rest of the night. "You must be as exhausted as everyone."

"That I am. It has been a hard time here. Everyone loves the duke and duchess, and the thought of losing her and what that would do to him . . . Well, thank the good Lord she is all right."

Barbara sat down and looked at her old friend. Even by candlelight she could see how pale Judith was. Every freckle stood out and there were deep blue shadows under her eyes. At one point, just before dawn, her fingers moved on the covers, as though searching for something. Barbara slipped her hand over them and Judith's became still, as though she had found the comfort she sought.

As the sun rose and the room became lighter, Barbara, who had dozed off, felt a faint pressure on her hand. She opened her eyes and saw that Judith was awake and smiling at her.

"Barbara," she whispered. "I thought you were at Arundel."

"Hush, don't talk, Judith. I came home yesterday and we set out immediately."

Judith ran her tongue over her cracked lips, and before she could mouth the word, Barbara had lifted her up, and taking the glass of water from the nightstand, poured it gently into her mouth.

"I am so thirsty."

"I can imagine."

"And so weak," protested Judith. "I can't even lift my hand to help you."

"Evidently you lost a lot of blood, Judith. I think we are very lucky to have you still with us," said Barbara with tears in her eyes.

"The baby is still all right, isn't he? The doctor told me he thought he would survive, but I haven't seen him," fretted Judith.

"As far as I know you are both out of danger, dearest. Now why don't you close your eyes . . ."

"And Simon. Where is Simon? Oh, God, he must be exhausted too. He was with me the whole time, Barbara."

Barbara was starting to explain that he was sound asleep when she heard a sound at the door. Simon was standing there, looking more like a released criminal than the Duke of Sutton.

"Is that you, Barbara? Is she awake?"

"Yes, Simon, awake and asking for you." Barbara got up and stepped away from the bed as Simon moved toward it like a sleepwalker. He was so tired that his usual skill at getting around had deserted him, and he bumped into the foot of the bed. Barbara saw Judith wince as the bed shook, but her friend bit back a groan and reached out her arms toward her husband.

Simon sat down on the edge of the bed and found his wife's face. "Oh, God, Judith, had I lost you . . ." His voice cracked and he buried his face in his wife's shoulder and sobbed. Judith slowly and gently stroked his head, her face flushed with color, as love lent her a moment of strength.

Barbara's eyes filled with tears and she was about to excuse herself when she realized that neither would have heard her anyway. Simon and Judith's emotion was so naked and so intimate that Barbara left quickly, moved to her core by the strength of their feelings. As she walked down the hall, she felt a mixture of sadness and relief. Relief that Simon and Judith had not lost each other and sadness because she wondered if the feelings of affection and attraction she had for Wardour would ever grow into the love that existed between her friends.

25

"Where is the baby, Mrs. Dunsmore?" Barbara asked the housekeeper when she had found her.

"He is with a wet nurse in the green bedroom, Lady Barbara."

"May I see him? And perhaps bring him in to his mother in a little while? I think she will rest easier if she sees for herself that he is all right."

"Of course, Lady Barbara."

Barbara let herself quietly into the bedroom. The wet nurse had just finished feeding the baby and had put him down to sleep. Barbara leaned over his cradle and marveled that a human being could be so tiny.

"He is a fighter, my lady, even though he is so small. His sucking gets stronger at every feeding."

"May I bring him up to his mother?"

"Of course."

Barbara lifted the little flannel-clad bundle and had a fleeting image of herself lifting her own child someday. She stroked the teeny head. "Another redhead, like his sister." Her fantasy child had red hair too, she realized, as she carried the baby down the hall.

Judith was slightly propped up on her pillows and Simon was sitting next to her, his hand in hers. When Barbara entered with the baby in her arms, Judith pulled herself up and Simon immediately protested. "You must not exert yourself, Judith."

"It is the baby, Simon. Barbara is bringing the baby."

"Are you sure you are strong enough?"

"Oh, yes. Just let me hold him for a few minutes, please."

Barbara placed the "heir-apparent" in her friend's arms.

"He is so small!" exclaimed Judith. "Has he nursed?"

"He had just finished when I went up," Barbara replied.

"I won't have any milk for a few days." Judith sighed. "The doctor warned me, but I want to feed him myself."

"Don't fret, Judith," said Simon. Judith pulled the blanket down from the baby's head and Simon traced his son's crumpled features with one finger.

"He is a tiny scrap, isn't he? He has some hair, I see. What color is it?"

"Red."

Simon laughed.

"Do you have a name for him yet?" Barbara asked.

"We had decided to name him after two fine men of our acquaintance," Simon told her. "Robert Francis Ballance."

"Robin and Francis will both be honored."

"It is hard to imagine that this is the future Duke of Sutton," whispered Judith.

"We all come into the world the same, don't we," mused Simon. "Although not all so hazardously."

"May I bring Sophy in for just a few minutes?"

Judith's face lit up. "Oh, would you, Barbara? How is she?"

"She has been a very brave little girl. You have a lot to be proud of."

"And thankful for," said Judith.

As soon as it was apparent, after a few days, that Judith and the baby were doing well, Robin and Diana said their good-byes and returned to Ashurst. Barbara stayed, partly to help out with Sophy, but more to renew her relationship with her old friend. She and Judith spent hours sitting quietly in the garden while the baby nursed and slept and Judith regained her strength. At first they said little, for both were just content to be in one another's company.

"Everything looks new to me, Barbara," said Judith one day. "I am so happy we are both alive, little Robin and I, that I just want to sit for hours, drinking it all in."

Later in her visit, however, Judith asked about Barbara's time at Arundel. "Did you feel at home there, Barbara? And what is his mother like?"

"I felt quite at home after only a few days. It is a beautiful house and close to the sea, which means there are lovely breezes even on the hottest of days. And Lady Wardour couldn't have been kinder. She spent a lot of time teaching me about the house and is already planning her move to the dower house. Although she is so easy to get along with, I will be pleased to be on my own."

"She sounds an exemplary mother-in-law!" said Judith.

"Yes, and Wardour is an exemplary son and landlord, which I had already guessed."

"So you are quite happy with your choice, then, Barbara?"

"Yes, yes, I think I am," Barbara answered slowly.

"You sound as though you have a reservation or two."

"Oh, Judith, I sometimes am not sure I know what love is or is supposed to be."

"I don't know that anyone does," said Judith with a smile.

"Oh, you and Simon certainly do," replied Barbara, with a trace of the old resentment in her voice.

"Of course we love one another, but it is not all sweetness and light as it appears on the outside, Barbara. Simon has times when he is as distant as in the old days. And times of anger too. Sometimes I feel resentful that we will never be able to ride or dance or walk together in a normal, carefree manner. And one of the most difficult parts of this marriage," continued Judith with a shaky laugh, "is probably the most trivial. I am not, you may recall, the most tidy of individuals."

Barbara smiled, remembering how Judith could sit and read or draw, oblivious to any disarray around her.

"Well, *everything* must be in its place for Simon to be independent. I can never just relax. I must always be worrying about chairs being in place and brushes set out exactly so on the dressing table. And I feel so terribly selfish at times when I just want to sit quietly in front of the fire, reading to myself while my husband does likewise. If I am reading, I feel as though I'm shutting Simon out. And yet there are times when I want to. Shut him out, that is, and not always be thinking about him. Oh, dear, I don't know what started me off," confessed Judith. "I am sorry to burden you."

"Don't apologize, Judith. I am happy you told me. I am not happy there are those tensions, of course, but I have a confession to make too. I have been quite jealous at times, because you seemed so perfectly happy. You chatter on to Miranda as though it were all sweetness and light. I've been resentful because the two of you have a life I couldn't share. And you seemed to have a new friend who took the place of an old one," Barbara admitted in a low voice.

"Oh, Barbara, did you feel shut out? I am so sorry. Miranda could never replace you. You should know that. But indeed, how could you?" continued Judith thoughtfully. "You are right. It is very easy for married women to become caught up in conversation about teething and first words . . ."

"The length of a first labor . . ."

"You have felt neglected. Oh, my dearest friend, I should have known."

"No, Judith, I should have said something a long time ago."

"Nonsense. We must have another promise of undying friendship as we did at Mrs. Hastings' Academy."

Barbara laughed. "We were an idealistic duo, weren't we, in those days? Plans to pursue our art together. Marriage only if we could find someone who respected our minds. But yes, let us promise not to let the concerns of grown-up life distance us too much."

"And keep us from intimate talks. For no matter how much I love Simon and no matter how easily he and I can open our minds to one another, there is nothing like a talk with a good friend. I have missed you, Barbara, and I am ashamed to admit that I didn't know how much until now." Judith reached over and took Barbara's hand. The two women sat there quietly, enjoying a closeness that needed no words.

26

Barbara broke the silence after a few minutes. She had been looking at the sundial without really seeing it, when her gaze was caught by the dark green plants around its base. They were myrtle plants.

"You know, Judith, according to one Madame Zenobia, I will not marry Wardour after all."

"Madame Zenobia?"

"A gypsy woman who was at our Midsummer Fair. There is an old custom, you see. You place a piece of myrtle in the pages of your prayer book and sleep with it under your pillow. If the myrtle is still there in the morning, the marriage will never take place."

"And you did it, and of course the myrtle was still there," teased Judith.

"Well, yes."

"You are not having second thoughts because of that, are you? Your visit sounds as if it was delightful."

"Not really second thoughts so much as what I said earlier. How does one know love? There certainly is respect and affection and physical attraction between me and Peter."

"Well, it sounds as if all the right ingredients are present. Did you enjoy his kisses?"

"Now, I didn't *say* he kissed me, Judith," Barbara replied with mock dignity. "But yes, he did, and yes, I enjoyed them very much. In fact, I wanted them to go on longer, but he was very respectful and restrained."

"Hmmm. A good sign on your side. I'm not sure if it is on his, however," teased Judith.

"But there is something else, Judith, which I am ashamed to even tell you about."

"And what is that?"

"There was a fiddler at the midsummer celebrations."

"Yes?"

"A Scotsman who is the most talented musician I have ever heard."

"But what does he have to do with you and Wardour?"

"I felt a kind of joy in his presence that I have not felt in a long time, not even with Peter."

"Most probably it was only the music. You are always responsive to anyone with talent."

"I think that is part of it. But it also has something to do with his twinkling blue eyes and sense of humor. And his legs."

"His legs! When did you see his legs, may I ask?"

Barbara giggled. "He wore a kilt, my dear, and he had bonnie strong legs covered with the same auburn hair as he has on his head. Do you not think one should be able to ask to see one's intended husband's legs, to make sure they can compete with another's?"

Judith looked over at Barbara and they both began to laugh helplessly.

"You are shameless, Barbara."

"Well, it is amusing, and then again it is not. I met him, quite by chance, the morning after the fair. And then, out of the blue, there he was at Arundel. Peter hired him to play. We played together, Judith."

Barbara's voice had become quite serious and Judith felt a pang of uneasiness.

"You have played with others before," she responded evenly, not showing her concern.

"But never with someone who was so talented. The music flowed and blended in a way I cannot describe. And he can go from Mozart to a reel with ease."

"But he is only a hired musician, Barbara," Judith reminded her gently. "Not someone you will ever see again."

"I know. I did a foolish thing, though," admitted Barbara.

"You didn't let him kiss you!"

"No. Although I wanted him to desperately. Even more than I ever wanted Peter to kiss me."

"Well, it is quite possible to be attracted to an inappropriate person, as we both know. But what did you do?"

"I referred him to David Treves as a possible patron. I did it without thinking, but now I am sure I did it so I would at least have some news of him."

"Well, he may never make his way to London at all."

"That is true. But you see, Judith, I don't know if then I would be more relieved or disappointed."

"From everything you have told me, my dear, everything you want and need you will find with Wardour. Do not torture yourself wondering whether it is 'true love.' That is something two people create together after marriage."

"You are no doubt right, Judith. With Peter I will have everything I could want." Except music and joy, she thought to herself.

27

While Barbara was renewing her friendship with Judith, Alec was making his way slowly to London. August was harvest time, and there were plenty of harvest-home celebrations at which he could take in a generous amount.

After fiddling late into the evening, he would often treat himself to a glass of cider or ale at the local tavern, and if he was lucky, after playing a few soft airs, fiddle his way to a bed or a place in the barn, which saved him from sleeping outside.

On this particular evening, in the White Horse Tavern, it was clear he was unlikely to fiddle his way anywhere, since there was another busker there before him. But he had made enough in the past few days to pay for a room on his own, so he decided to keep his own instrument out of sight and sit back and enjoy someone else for a change.

The fiddler was an older man, likely in his late fifties, and much the worse for wear and alcohol, if the veins on his nose and his reddening eyes were anything to go by. His hands shook as he pulled out his fiddle, but as soon as he drew the bow across the strings, they were as steady as Alec's own.

He played a few old songs and a slow air and then began to sing. His voice was rough but true, and although he often stopped to wet his throat, the ale just sweetened his music. As he got drunker, the songs got bawdier. Alec thought to himself that there was much more fun in the bawdiness found in taverns than in the debaucheries of the upper class.

Just as the man finished a particularly amusing ditty, the barkeep announced closing time. "Ye know if ye don't get home soon, Tom, your old woman will be here to drag ye there herself."

"Just one more, and this one of my own making," said Tom, winking at Alec, who grinned back. "This one's for me wife."

Alec expected another bawdy song, and was surprised to realize that Tom had written a love song. A rough song in which he humorously insulted his wife, but a moving one despite that. Or perhaps because of it, thought Alec as he listened to the chorus. He must have had too much ale, he thought, if he had tears coming to his eyes at such a song, but it was long-lasting love that the old man was singing about. Unbidden, the image of Lady Barbara came to mind, a woman as unlike the old woman in the song as could be found, and he smiled to himself. Imagine singing such a song to her. But he *could* imagine it. He could easily imagine himself inviting her to sit herself down upon his knee, feeling the joy in their closeness, just as he felt joy in his music. For what had brought tears to his eyes was a yearning for a lifelong partner in a woman who meant as much to him as his music. The song had made it clear to him that he wanted Barbara Stanley, that he knew they could have joined their lives as easily and as equally as they had joined their instruments.

But to her he was only a wandering Scotsman. And she was to marry the marquess in the fall. . . .

The barkeep was tapping him on the shoulder, jolting him out of his reverie. "It is closing time, but surely no reason for looking that sad," he joked.

"Have you got a bed for the night?"

"Show me your money and I have."

Alec handed him a few shillings for the ale and for the room, and the man pointed in the direction of the stairs.

"Up there and second door to your right. Ye'll find it is clean enough."

Alec lifted his pack and carried it up to the small bedroom. It was clean and surprisingly comfortable. Although any bed would be more comfortable than a hayloft or a hillside, he thought. I'll be glad to get to London and have regular baths and clean sheets. I must call on this Sir David Treves, he decided as he drifted off. I have to survive two months in London, and it will surely be easier with a patron. And perhaps I'll get to see ma' braw bonnie lassie again.

Perhaps it was the bawdy songs, but Alec spent the night dreaming of a very different Barbara than the one he had come to know. A Barbara who sat herself down on his knees and ran her hand down his leg, discovering his skean dhu, and then ran her hand up under his kilt to see if he had any other hidden weapons. He woke several times during the night, mad with frustrated desire. "I will no be able to stand it, lass, if ye keep torturing me like this," he said to her in one dream, just as Barbara kissed him full on the lips. "Ah, no, my dear," his dream Barbara said with the sweetest smile, "for don't you know I mean no harm to you? I love you most of all."

28

By the time Alec got to London, it was mid-September and he only had five weeks to go until he won his wager and presented himself at his grandfather's door. The duke could be in town, but there was no chance at all of their meeting. Even were he to be hired to play for a ball or musicale, his grandfather was unlikely to be present, since he attended as few social functions as he could, leaving them to his son and daughter-in-law the years that they came with him. This year, Alec knew, his father was remaining in Scotland.

Alec arrived in London late in the afternoon and was turned away from a few places because of his appearance before he found decent lodgings. He paid for a week in advance and then counted his money. He had decided to invest in one good suit of clothes, which would leave him with only enough to eat sparsely for a week. But it was a necessary investment, for in London he needed to hire himself out rather than work the streets. And, he had to confess, he was getting tired of busking. In the country, in warm weather, it was delightful to travel willy-nilly, following fairs, sleeping outdoors, waking to the gurgle of a brook and the sounds of birds. In London, performing on the street meant leaving comfortable, clean lodgings and being wakened by flea bites, not bird song.

During his first day, he therefore visited a tailor and shoemaker. The fit of the suit hardly rivaled Weston's, but at least it would look better than what he had. And any shoes would be better than his worn-out silver-buckled brogues. He inquired casually about Sir David Treves, assuming that as a member of the *ton*, he would be known for *something*, scandalous or otherwise. He drew blanks at a few coffeehouses and rude stares when he ventured into Mayfair to knock at back entrances and question the servants. Finally one cook, who was from Scotland, was able to tell him that there was a Joshua Treves, a Jew, who owned a shipping business and whose office was by the docks. She knew this, she said, because her brother was a docksman, and when she visited him, she had noticed the name. Alec thanked her for her information and for the scones she insisted on feeding him at the kitchen table.

He decided to go straight to the docks, and found the office without too much trouble. He asked the front-room clerk if he might find Sir David Treves here.

The clerk looked him up and down, and Alec gripped his bonnet in his hands, as though holding tightly onto that would help him keep his temper.

"And what business would you have with Sir David, may I ask?"

"I was recommended to him by a friend of his. He won't recognize me by name, but if you tell him that Lady Barbara Stanley sent me, I am sure he will see me."

The clerk was suitably impressed by the Stanley name, and asked Alec to wait a minute. He emerged from the rear a few minutes later with a tall, dark young man whose exquisitely tailored bottle-green coat and fawn trousers made Alec feel like a wild Highlander in his patched kilt.

Sir David, for so he assumed it was, looked at him inquiringly. "You know Lady Barbara Stanley?"

Alec inclined his head. "Yes, Sir David. We met at Ashurst and then again at Arundel. I am a musician, you see, and she said you were a music lover and something of a patron. I was hoping I might find employment during the Little Season."

David smiled. "If Lady Barbara recommended you, then

you must be good. But I fear there are not too many places in London where they demand Scottish reels. I don't think I can help you. I am sorry."

"But there are places for a violinist to play Bach and Mozart for private entertainments, and waltzes and country dances at a ball, are there not? Could you recommend me?"

"That depends, Mr. . . ?"

"Gower. Alec Gower. From Scotland."

"So I gathered," said David, with another smile and a glance down at the kilt.

"Ach, aye, weel, ma new suit of clothes was juist no ready yet," replied Alec with a grin.

"You have a very flexible accent, Mr. Gower."

"Aye, and my music is just as flexible, I assure you. I brought my instrument with me. I will play a little, if you like. I know I would not feel comfortable recommending anyone without hearing him."

"All right. Come back to my office, Mr. Gower, and I will hear a little Mozart."

Alec followed him and drew out his violin. "I will give you Eine Kleine Nachtmusik, even though it is daytime," he joked, and played the first movement. Although it was only one part, the Scotsman played so well that David hardly missed the rest of the orchestra. He was good, and David was filled with admiration and envy.

"That was excellent, Mr. Gower. Now why don't you play me a country tune so I can hear your other voice."

Alec played him a lilting waltz, and then the lament he had played for Barbara.

David was silent for a moment or two after the last notes faded. "I am ashamed to confess I have tears in my eyes from that last tune, Mr. Gower. It reminds me of some of our more melancholy Ladino songs."

"Aye, it is a lament. And it is not surprising that the music of one dispossessed people should resemble another."

David's eyebrows lifted in surprise.

"Well," Alec explained, "many a Highlander has been forced into exile by the clearances. And both our tongue and our plaids have been forbidden us at one time or another."

"That is true. I had forgotten. But it is rare to find such sympathy and understanding."

"I would like to hear some of your music, Sir David. That is, if you are content to hire me or recommend me."

"Oh, I think I can find you work," said David. "It is only the Little Season, but I will be holding a few musical evenings myself, and I have enough contacts in the *ton* that my name will mean something at a few doors. And once a door or two is opened to you, the word will spread."

"I am very grateful, Sir David."

"No need to be. I am the one who should thank Lady Barbara for sending you my way. Did you have a chance to hear her play?"

"As a matter of fact, we played together at Arundel."

"Now, that must have been a rare treat for both you and the audience."

"Aye, it was indeed," said Alec quietly.

"She will be in Town for part of the Season until her wedding. Perhaps you will have a chance to play together again."

"Perhaps," replied Alec noncommittally.

"Here is my card, Mr. Gower. Come and see me at my home in a few days' time, and I should have several engagements set up for you."

The clerk looked up in surprise and distaste as Sir David shook hands with the Scotsman at the door. Sir David was somewhat eccentric, he thought, when it came to music, and he went back to his accounts with a sigh of disapproval.

29

David had taken Deborah out for several short drives after their outing to Kew Gardens, but Sarah's presence made any sort of intimacy impossible, a fact that both were paradoxically grateful for and frustrated by. David was beginning to feel that his presence was pointless. If his motive was only a charitable one, he could just send his groom. And if he was motivated by desire, then being with Deborah only made him realize his desire could never be satisfied.

He decided, therefore, not to continue the acquaintance, but thought it only fair to inform Deborah personally of his reasons, and to assure her that his carriage would still be available. And so, after hesitating for several days, he made his way to Mitre Street one Friday afternoon. As he came in sight of the Cohens', he met Malachi hurrying up the street.

"Business was not good today, my friend? I see you still have oranges to sell. Shouldn't you be haunting the theaters tonight?"

Malachi looked at him with a puzzled and rather shocked expression on his face.

"Tonight, Sir David? Why, of course I couldn't be selling tonight. It is almost the Sabbath."

"Of course, I wasn't thinking at all," replied David, shamefacedly.

"Do you not observe the Sabbath?"

"My grandfather did so religiously, my father irregularly, and I, I must confess, have never given much thought to it.

But that is not true of all of us Sephardim, as well you know. Bevis Marks is a most active synagogue."

"I am not a very religious man, Sir David, nor is Mr. Cohen. But there is something about the Sabbath meal and the day of rest that give meaning to the hard week coming."

"Well, I hope I am early enough to talk to Miss Cohen for a few minutes."

"You'd better hurry, lad. She'll have helped her father close the store by now, and she and Sarah have been cooking all day."

"I'll go ahead of you, then," apologized David, as he hurried up to the door.

Sarah answered his knock. "Sir David! I couldn't imagine who it could be before supper. Did Miss Deborah invite you?"

"No, no, Sarah. I just wanted to talk with her for a few minutes."

"I'll go get 'er, but ye truly only 'ave a minute or two," said Sarah, pointing to the last streaks of sunlight on the horizon.

Deborah hurried to the door when she received the summons, wondering what on earth had brought David Treves to their house on a Sabbath evening. She was annoyed with him for interrupting her last-minute preparations, and annoyed with herself for the way her heart lifted when she heard his name.

"What can I do for you, Sir David?"

David looked down at her. As the sunset struck the windows of the houses they turned to gold, illuminating Deborah's face and creating an aureole of her hair. She was beautiful, this Deborah Cohen, thought David.

"I had hoped for a few minutes alone with you, but I am ashamed to confess I had forgotten you would be busy with Sabbath preparations. I will come back another time."

"You could stay," she answered a bit sharply.

"Is that an invitation, Miss Cohen? You don't sound that

welcoming," he teased. "And I shouldn't like to intrude," he added more seriously.

"Please join us in our Sabbath meal, Sir David," said Deborah in softer tones. "I will have no time to talk to you, but at least I can repay some of your generosity to us."

"All right, I will, and thank you."

"Come in, come in, then. It is almost time to gather and light the candles."

Although the Treveses no longer regularly celebrated the Sabbath, David had been to Shabbat meals at friends' houses. But those elaborately laid-out tables in fashionable Sephardic homes had not opened to him the meaning behind the Sabbath as much as the Cohens' simple table did. Upon the spotless white tablecloth was the Kiddush cup and the wine and a golden loaf of challah. Deborah lit the candles just moments before the sun set and, closing her eyes, uttered the traditional blessing.

Malachi and Sarah stood silent as Mr. Cohen recited the praise of a valiant woman, then filled the cups and recited Kiddush over the wine. They all drank. Then he repeated the blessing over the bread and they all ate. And then the real meal began, a simple but delicious feast.

David had had his eyes on Deborah as she bent over the candles and during her father's recitation. As he heard the ancient words of praise, he thought how appropriate they were, for here was a valiant woman indeed. He thought of why he had come: to tell her good-bye, and realized that never to see her again would be impossible. In fact, Sir David Treves, the agnostic Jew, was imagining what it would be like to have Deborah lighting their own Sabbath candles every week, with him saying the blessing on their children who stood around the table. He did not only desire her, he realized. He loved her. And as he watched her lifting the wine to her lips, he murmured a special blessing of his own, to Whoever or Whatever in the universe had prompted him to bring Malachi home. Blessed are you, he thought, Creator of Deborah Cohen. Perhaps he was being blasphemous, since he didn't really believe, but David didn't care. Someone should be thanked for her presence. The question now for him was how to insure her presence in his life.

30

By the time Barbara arrived in London, Alec had already played several engagements arranged by David. These served their purpose, for once he was heard, hostesses made sure to pass the word about the talented Scots fiddler.

David had of course been present on some of these evenings, and during the intermissions, he would go up and further his acquaintance with Alec. David, although he played no instrument, was as great a music lover as Gower and could converse knowledgeably. After one such evening, when both of them had had a bit more to drink than usual, the two of them made their way home together, trading songs in Gaelic and Ladino. Alec's voice was pleasant, but nothing to compare to David's tenor. The first time the Scotsman heard it, he stopped in the middle of the street and grabbed his new friend by the sleeve.

"You did not tell me, laddie, that you are indeed a musician."

"No, no," protested David.

"Ah, but the voice is an instrument too, and yours is glorious."

David blushed and protested and they linked arms and proceeded down the street singing "The Isle of St. Helena."

It was natural, therefore, when David planned a dinner and musical interlude for a small group of friends, that he engage Alec's services for an evening whose guests included the Vanes and Lady Barbara Stanley.

This time Alec was not sent downstairs to eat with the servants. He was seated next to Nora and across from Barbara.

Barbara had been taken completely by surprise by his presence. She had been hoping that she would hear of Mr. Gower through David, but had never expected to encounter him so soon. She had smiled politely and mumbled something about being happy to see that Mr. Gower had made David's acquaintance, but was only too glad not to be required to converse with him. After her talk with Judith, she had resolved to put him out of her mind as an aberration or momentary distraction from her love for Wardour. Certainly a woman was allowed to find an attractive man attractive, without being accused . . . Well, no one was accusing her of anything, after all. And no matter that Mr. Gower could enjoy a taste of social equality with a host like David and a small and liberal guest list, he was not someone who could be considered seriously, even if she were free, which she was not.

And yet, having sorted all that through in her mind, she could not keep her eyes off his long, slender fingers wrapped around the stem of his wineglass, or the way the Prussian-blue coat complemented his eyes. Later, after Alec had played a Bach sonata, it was even harder to keep her mind off him. It was only because she responded to his music, she kept telling herself. But when David requested a duet, Barbara refused graciously but firmly. She could not risk another such experience and maintain a sensible distance.

"Do you sing for us instead, David," she requested. "Mr. Gower can accompany you."

"We *have* been practicing," replied Gower, with a mischievous glint in his eye, and played one of David's Ladino songs. After that, David sang "Gile Mar" to the haunting accompaniment of Alec's violin.

"That last brought tears to my eyes," said Nora. "Can you tell us what it was about? I would guess lost love."

"I am not sure it would be wise to translate it, Lady Vane, even in this company," replied Alec. "It could be heard as the lament of a woman for a man, but the woman, in this case, is Ireland, and the man Charles Stuart."

"As a Northumbrian bred and born, I have always been rather partial to the Stuarts, Mr. Gower. No wonder I loved your song."

Just before she left, Barbara went up to Gower, who was packing his violin away.

"I am glad you were able to make contact with Sir David, Mr. Gower. I hope your time in London is profitable."

"It has been so far, my lady. I thank you for recommending me."

"It was the least I could do for such a talented musician," Barbara replied, feeling like they both were only uttering platitudes. But what else was there to say to this man, after all?

Alec was equally disturbed. For almost another month he was Alec Gower, the fiddler, and not Lord Alexander MacLeod. He could not call on Barbara and he would only see her by chance, when he happened to be playing at a social gathering she was attending. They were not in an enchanted copse where a mere busker could brush the lips of a lady with his fingertips. They were in London, where he might, on a rare occasion such as this, sit at the same table, but most certainly not have the opportunity to put his arm around her in another waltz. And by the time he could assume his own identity, she would be married to Wardour.

"Bloody hell," he muttered as he fumbled with his violin case.

"I beg your pardon, Mr. Gower?" Barbara asked, not sure what she had just heard.

"I jammed ma' finger, lass, that is all," he lied.

"Let me see," said Barbara, with the musician's instant concern for hands and fingers.

Alec stuck his hand out without thinking, and then almost laughed out loud as Barbara inspected it. "I see nothing amiss, Mr. Gower," she announced.

The touch of Barbara's thumb running down each finger was an exquisite torture. As for Barbara, not only did she see nothing amiss, she could not help admiring, from close up, the slender fingers and muscular hand partially covered with red hair and freckles. There was both strength and sensitivity in such a hand, and she stood there, aware of the same current that had run between them at Ashurst.

"I need ma hand back, lass."

Barbara blushed unbecomingly red and dropped his hand as if it were the source of her hot embarrassment. It had certainly been the source of another kind of warmth that she didn't even want to think about.

"I am glad to see there is no injury, Mr. Gower. It was good to hear you play again. Good night."

She was gone in a second and Alec cursed again, this time longer and harder, at the thought of his bonnie lassie in the arms of another man. He was almost tempted to go after her and confess, here and now, who he was. But if he did that, he would lose his chance at music, and without his music he was nothing and had nothing to offer her anyway. And so he swallowed the words and some brandy and got himself home to bed.

31

Deborah Cohen spent the days after David's Sabbath visit alternating between daydreaming about him and scolding herself for her own unrealistic expectations. He had made it clear to her that he respected her too much to make her his mistress and not enough to make her his wife. She had made it clear that she *was* respectable. All too clear. Why should he come back? Why had he come that Friday? Deborah prided herself on her account-keeping, but had to rip two pages out of the ledger that week, she was so distracted.

Her father had quietly asked her about Sir David's intentions.

"I do not think his interest goes beyond friendship, Father," she told him.

"And are you disappointed, my dear?"

"Perhaps a little," admitted Deborah.

"Sir David is a very attractive young man," observed her father as offhandedly as he could.

"Yes, but we have little in common, Father. I am a merchant's daughter."

"And he is a merchant's son," Mr. Cohen reminded her. "The Treveses are in trade also, Deborah, don't forget that."

"But his family socializes with gentry. And he was granted a baronetcy."

"It took three generations to achieve that, Deborah. And

you are both Jewish. I would not be happy to see you marry a Christian."

"There has been no mention of marriage with anyone, I can assure you, Father," replied Deborah with her old tartness.

"Or any other arrangement, I trust."

"David has always acted towards me with the greatest respect. You know, there are some ways in which David hardly seems Jewish," continued Deborah.

"The Sephardim have always been very accomplished at blending in, Deborah, wherever they have lived, and they have done the same thing here. Or the wealthy ones have," he added. "Jews from Poland and other countries . . . well, we have had the ghettoes and pogroms to remind us who we are. But although he stumbled a bit on the blessings, I think he is more Jewish than you think. Why would he be haunting the house of a pretty girl like Deborah Cohen and not some English girl?"

Deborah blushed.

"Well, time will tell. For my part, I would have no objection. You deserve more of the good things in life, and I have never wanted you to marry someone only to bring him into the business."

David had said nothing when he had left the house, so Deborah half expected him never to call again and half hoped he would knock at the door at any minute. By Wednesday, however, she had reached a state of numbness, not quite ready to open herself to the thought of never seeing him again. When he appeared early that afternoon, therefore, he was met by Deborah at her most prickly.

"May I take you for a ride this afternoon, Miss Cohen?" he politely requested.

"I am busy, Sir David. It is a shame you did not let me know earlier."

"It was a busy week for me too, but I should have gotten

you word despite that. I apologize. But can I persuade you to spare me a little time?"

"Sarah is not available, Sir David, so it will have to be another time."

"I am glad that Sarah is not here to be disappointed," said David, "'for I would have asked her to stay behind. I want to speak with you alone."

Deborah started to object and David quickly assured her that they would not go far and they he would return her at any time she wanted. "You have nothing to fear, Miss Cohen."

Deborah at once felt ridiculous. He wasn't taking her out to proposition her, he was taking her out to say good-bye. He was a kind man, and instead of just never coming back, he was going to end their friendship gently. I can at least be quiet and dignified, she thought, and agreed to accompany him.

After David lifted her into the carriage, they sat silently as the groom drove them out of the East End. "I thought we would not go far, just to Hyde park, Miss Cohen," announced David, breaking the silence.

Deborah looked startled. "Isn't it a rather fashionable hour for that, Sir David?"

"It is a bit early, so our pace will be above a crawl, I hope," he replied with a smile.

"It was not speed I was concerned about. I am hardly dressed appropriately," complained Deborah.

"You look lovely, Miss Cohen." And indeed she did, dressed in her second-best muslin, a sea-foam green that complemented her coloring.

"But my hair . . ."

"Is glorious," said David, reaching out to gently brush a strand back from her face. Deborah shivered.

"Are you cold, Miss Cohen?" he asked with concern.

"No, not cold . . . just nervous."

"Miss Cohen, I have a request to make."

"Yes?"

"May I call you Deborah and will you call me David?"

Why on earth does he ask that now? she wondered.

"Don't you think it is foolish to be on a first-name basis only to say good-by?" she blurted out.

"Good-bye? I am not intending to say good-bye, I assure you, Miss Cohen."

"Oh. Then why did you call for me?"

"I called on you for several reasons. To confirm our friendship. To introduce you to some friends. And for something else."

Deborah blushed, and cursed herself for speaking without thinking. He would now feel she had put him on the spot.

"Aren't you at all curious about my third reason, Deborah? There, I've assumed your permission."

"Oh, call me Deborah, by all means. I suppose a mistress would be on first-name terms with her lover."

"Good God, woman. Will you get that idea out of your head? I did not call on you to give you a slip on the shoulder. I called on you to ask you to marry me."

Deborah was speechless.

"Well, no, that isn't really what I had planned to do," David said more calmly. "I was going to ask you, very respectfully and politely, if we might expand our friendship into something more serious. Then I was going to court you, then speak to your father in the approved manner, and *then* ask you to marry me. But you are like a hedgehog, and have spoiled all my careful planning. So tell me, Deborah Cohen," said David, putting his finger on her chin and turning her face to meet his, "would you consider marrying me?"

Deborah opened her mouth to speak, but nothing came out.

"Speechless, Deborah?" teased David. "A first. But are you speechless with surprise or outrage?"

"I don't know what to say, Sir David."

"Please call me David."

"You know I have enjoyed your companionship."

"Yes?"

"And you know that I find you very attractive . . ."

"But . . .?"

"Are you sure you wish to court plain Deborah Cohen from the East End when you could probably find yourself the daughter of an earl?"

"Do you mean, do I want a Jewish woman for my wife?"

"I suppose that is part of what I am asking, David. There is not only a difference in our stations, but also in the way we think about ourselves as Jews. I suspect that had you not met me, you may well have married a Christian lady. I would never have married a Christian gentleman."

"You may be right, Deborah. I confess that although I have not been eager to rush into it, I may well have ended up marrying an impoverished peer's daughter. But I have met you, and fallen in love with you. It would be foolish to deny that we have led different lives. But there is more than one way of being Jewish. You and your father are not extremely observant, although you are more so than my family."

"I just would never want to try to 'pass,' David. I am proud of who I am."

"Is that what you think I do? I assure you, unless you convert, and even then, you are always identified as a Jew, no matter how liberal the circles in which you move," replied David with a touch of bitterness.

"You have always seemed immune to that kind of prejudice, for you are very much the English gentleman."

"I confess that until the incident with Malachi, I tried to keep myself as unaware as possible. I had convinced myself that the less people thought of me as a Jew, the better chance I had at working for reforms."

"With me as your wife, you will hardly blend in, David," said Deborah, wanting with all her heart to accept him, but not willing to gloss over the difficulties.

"Oh, I can tell them you're Irish!" he teased. "With that

red hair and those freckles, you could well be. Although, as Miss Cohen, you are probably as acceptable as a Miss O'Toole. It is hard to say whether anti-Jewish or anti-Irish sentiment is more virulent."

"David . . ."

"Yes, Deborah?"

"I would like two things."

"Anything."

"I would like to give a 'yes' to the question you intended to ask me. I would like to be courted."

"Done. I never wanted to rush you. And the other?"

"I would like you to kiss me."

"Nothing would delight me more," David replied with great formality. He leaned down and quietly touched her lips.

"I am afraid there is one other thing," said Deborah a moment after his brief kiss.

"Yes?"

"Give me a real kiss, David."

David touched her lips again, gently at first, and then hungrily as he felt her response. When they at last pulled away from one another, they were immediately drawn back into another kiss.

David finally broke their embrace. "I think Richmond would have been a better choice for this afternoon, Deborah. We are almost to the park."

Deborah reached up to smooth her hair with shaking hands. "I did not realize kissing could be like that," she admitted shyly.

"Neither did I," said David, smiling at her. "I hope this courtship will be a relatively short one."

"Perhaps it will," said Deborah.

32

Both Deborah and David were dazed by the time they entered the park, but David still had enough presence of mind to greet several acquaintances with a wave of his hand. His face lit up, Deborah couldn't help noticing, when a statuesque blond pulled her horse over to the carriage and leaned down to say hello. It was clear that whoever Lady Barbara Stanley was, she knew David well and liked him even better. After her introduction to Deborah, Barbara made sure to include her in the conversation, but there was not much Deborah could add to the news of mutual acquaintances they were trading back and forth.

"Do you like music, Miss Cohen?" inquired Barbara.

"Why, yes I do," replied Deborah. "Very much."

"David, I am having a musical evening next week to welcome Wardour back to town. I have extended an invitation to the Duke of Wellington and I think he will attend. Perhaps Miss Cohen would like to be your guest?"

David assured her that they would both love to attend. "And speaking of music, Barbara, I do not think I ever thanked you for sending Alec Gower to me. I have enjoyed his company almost as must as his music. Will he be among the musicians?"

Barbara hesitated. It would indeed seem odd if she did not hire someone she herself had recommended. "Perhaps, if he has no other engagement."

"You must have him there if Wellington is to be present."

"I suppose I must, then," said Barbara with a smile. "Would you do me a favor and ask him?"

"Of course."

"It was delightful to meet you, Miss Cohen. I will be looking forward to seeing you again when we have more time for conversation. Good-bye, David."

As Barbara turned her mare and trotted away, David reached for Deborah's hand and said, "I am pleased I was able to introduce you. Lady Barbara is a good friend."

Deborah drew her hand away. "I could see that," she replied coolly.

"You did not like her, then?" asked David.

"I think the question is how much you like her. You seem very close."

"We became good friends almost immediately that we were introduced."

Deborah hated herself for asking, but couldn't help it. "Did neither of you want more than friendship? She would seem the perfect choice of bride for you. You move in the same circles, share a love of music . . ."

"Actually, Barbara is quite a talented musician herself."

"She would be," Deborah muttered, not quite under her breath.

"I beg your pardon?"

"Nothing. It is just that I am wondering whether you spent so much time with me this summer because Lady Barbara was out of town."

"As instantly as we became friends, Barbara and I agreed that we would not suit as anything else. Is it jealousy that is making you waspish, Deborah?"

Deborah's voice trembled as she answered. "If you wish to make a place in English society, it is clear that someone like Lady Barbara is more appropriate for you, David."

"Aside from the fact that we are not at all attracted to one another physically, Lady Barbara Stanley would never be allowed to marry a Jew. Her family is liberal, but not that liberal. And they are far from destitute. I have had a few chances already to marry into the ruined nobility, my dear, and have never even been tempted. Plain Miss Cohen is the bride I want."

"Plain Miss Cohen?"

"Your words, my dear, and I can see I will have to kiss you into submission again to convince you. But before I do, I want you to know that you are the equal of any woman I've ever met, titled or otherwise. I love *you*, my dear." And David leaned over and proceeded to prove it.

33

Barbara spent the next week alternating between nights at home to avoid a chance encounter with Mr. Gower and nights spent in a frenzy of activity to keep her mind off her musical evening. As it turned out, he was not playing for any of the events she attended. Why she had ever given him David's name, she didn't know. She *did* know. She *had* wanted to see him again. She still wanted to see him again, but it was a futile and shameful feeling, she told herself. Surely she had discovered that a quiet and steady affection seasoned with physical compatibility was what she wanted.

When Wardour finally arrived in London, his welcome was all that a prospective husband could wish for and more. If Barbara did not quite run to throw herself into his arms, neither did she wait for him to be shown into the morning room. She was in the hall just after he was announced, and the expression on her face was all that any fiancé could hope for.

"I am delighted to see you, Peter." Barbara drew him into the morning room and, shutting the door, lifted her face for a kiss.

Wardour bent down and gave her a gentle kiss. Surely the fact that I want him to kiss me more passionately is a sign that I am not lost, she thought. But why am I always left wanting more?

"I can only stay for a moment or two, but I wanted to see you," said Wardour. "I have to help Mother settle in. But we have an invitation to the Hardwicks' tonight. Will you be there?"

"I will be now," Barbara replied. "And my invitations? Did you receive them?"

"We did, and it sounds delightful, my dear. Until tonight." Wardour drew her into his arms for another kiss, one that was far more satisfactory, and Barbara decided that her doubts were just the normal pre-wedding nervousness.

Alec had spent the past week with one eye on his instrument and the other looking for Lady Barbara Stanley. He couldn't tell if he was disappointed or relieved when he found himself playing at a gathering that did not include her. Sir David was present on a few of these occasions, and always took time to come up to the musicians and chat with Alec for a few minutes.

"Are you engaged next Wednesday night?" David asked him the night after he had spoken with Barbara.

"No," said Alec. "Did you want me for the evening?"

"Actually, it is Lady Barbara who wishes to hire you."

Alec's face registered his surprise.

"I saw her in the park yesterday," explained David. "She is having a small gathering and would like you to come and play. The Duke of Wellington has been invited, so this is a great opportunity to demonstrate your talent."

"Wellington?"

"The Stanleys know him quite well. Major Stanley served under him at Waterloo."

Aye, and the Duke of Strathyre knows him very well also, thought Alec. He's only met me briefly, though, and I don't resemble my grandfather at all, so perhaps I will be safe. At any rate, it is too late to invent a previous engagement now.

"The duke used to play the violin, you know, and was supposed to be very talented."

"Then he will be a critical audience. I hope I don't disappoint him."

"I hardly think there is any danger of that, Alec. I will be looking forward to next week."

As I will not, thought Alec as he watched David return to his friends. Not only would he see Barbara, something he wanted and dreaded at the same time, but he would be risking exposure. It would be better to take the coward's way out and leave town, he thought.

But one week later he found himself knocking at the side entrance of the Stanley home, early enough to be introduced to the other musicians and become familiar with the acoustics of the music room. They were to play quartets this evening, and it did not seem that Lady Barbara would be playing. Alec was relieved that she would be safely in her place as hostess, which would keep distance between them. The other musicians were known to him and quite competent, but not of his caliber, and he carefully monitored his playing so he did not stand out for his superiority. It was something he was used to doing. It was something he had not had to do with Barbara, which had made playing with her such a joy.

The musicians were fed downstairs while the guests were enjoying their own dinner, so at least there was no fear of discovery over the soup or sweet, thought Alec. Perhaps he would be lucky and the duke would have forgotten him.

When the quartet entered the drawing room, the guests were still standing and chatting in small groups. Alec saw David looking down protectively at a small, red-haired woman whose dress was pretty, but by no means comparable to the gowns of the other women. He wondered who she was.

Wardour was there, of course, and his mother. They were in deep conversation with an elegant matron with raven-black hair, their backs to David and his companion. Barbara and her brother were talking to the duke and his wife.

If they all just sit down at once, I am safe for a while longer, thought Alec.

To his great relief they did. Major Stanley introduced the musicians, and they began to play.

After polite applause at the end of several pieces, Alec was optimistic. They would just finish their concert and pack up the instruments, and the guests would resume conversation. He wouldn't have to worry about the duke, and after tonight he would not see Barbara at close quarters again. And then he heard Lady Wardour chirping, "Peter, my dear, isn't that the Mr. Gower who played such a lovely duet with Barbara? Do see if we could get them to play that Mozart again."

Of course, once he had heard the story, Robin joined Lady Wardour in her request. The duke was nodding and smiling, and then looking at Alec with a crease between his eyes as though he was trying to place the talented Mr. Gower.

Alec let Barbara do the protesting. He was a hired musician, after all. If they had wanted him to play left-handed, he would have had to try.

Of course, she lost. The Vanes added their pleas, not having had the pleasure of hearing her play for so long. Robin had the fortepiano pushed out from the corner. And Barbara, her knees shaking, went up to Alec and apologized for imposing on him.

"I don't even know if I can get through it, Mr. Gower," she confessed in a low voice.

"Dinna fash yourself, lass," said Alec, knowing that would make her smile, which, thank God, it did, for how could they play Mozart, and her looking as if she'd lost her best friend? "What you forget, I'll remember, and vice versa. Once your fingers are on the keys, they will know what to do."

And indeed, after a few stumbles in the first measures, Barbara's fingers found their way and she lost herself in the music. They played even better than they had at Arundel, and she thought the sweetness of his playing would break her heart.

When the music ended, no one applauded. Alec and Barbara didn't even notice, for they were only aware of each other. They were two musicians, a man and a woman, playing two quite different instruments, and yet they had become one voice.

Wardour broke the spell when he got up and approached his fiancée. "That was quite wonderful, my dear. Almost as good as at Arundel."

Barbara gave him a dazed smile. It took her a moment or two to comprehend who he was and what he had said.

Wardour's move brought almost everyone up to the two to congratulate them. Deborah had not wanted to, but David grabbed her hand, and she shyly gave her compliments to Barbara while David shook Alec's hand. Barbara took Deborah's arm and moved away from the piano. "Come, sit down with me, Deborah, and tell me how you met David," she said, anxious to get away from the praise and from her acute consciousness of Alec's presence.

The duke was the only one who had remained in his seat. Alec had brought back memories of his childhood and youth. His father and he had both been talented amateurs, and occasionally, when he heard playing like this, he was filled with regret for what had been long gone from his life.

He finally unfolded himself from his chair and approached the Scotsman, who was, if he was not mistaken, the grandson of his old acquaintance, the Duke of Strathyre.

David turned and pulled Alec over to Wellington. "I would like to introduce you, your grace."

"No need," replied the duke. "I am quite sure this talented young man is—"

"Overwhelmed by the privilege of playing for you." Alec broke into the Duke's revelation and shook his hand with a bone-crushing strength while looking him pointedly in the eyes.

"Hmmm, yes, er, no, I am the one overwhelmed," replied the duke, now certain that this was indeed Alec MacLeod. It was clear that the young man did not want to be identified. David was looking at the duke and was surprised to see the sadness in his eyes as he continued his compliments.

"I used to play the violin, Mr.—?"

"Gower, your grace. I did not know that."

"Oh, yes. Music was my greatest love at one time. But when I realized that I would always be an amateur and needed to put my energy into a career, I burned my violin and haven't touched one since."

Involuntarily, Alec turned, as though to reassure himself that his own beloved instrument was safe.

"Yes," the duke continued, "I had to be quite ruthless. I have never regretted it, however, except on those rare occasions like tonight when I hear someone who has married his art rather than abandoning her, as it were. And yet music, I think, is not a career choice for a gentleman," he added, looking directly at Alec.

"It is not a usual one, your grace. But sometimes it is the music which chooses you."

"Well, I hope to hear you play again, Mr. . . . . Gower."

"Thank you, your grace."

As soon as the duke was out of earshot, David turned to Alec and said, "Now, who would have guessed that the Iron Duke played the violin once upon a time? And then just gave it up, like that."

"I can understand it," replied Alec. "If I could not have music as my life, I am not sure I would continue playing."

"You are lucky, then, to be free to choose."

Alec smiled to himself. He was lucky that his grandfather hadn't refused his wager. And he was lucky that he had silver in his pocket, enough to get home on and more.

"Aye, I am free to choose a part of my life," he answered, looking over at Barbara where she sat with Deborah. "What wonderful hair! I am always glad to see another redhead." He smiled. "One can always commiserate on the miserable childhoods we have had, being called 'carrot top' or 'red Alec.' "

"Come, let me introduce you to Miss Cohen."

Barbara sensed, rather than saw, Alec approach, and although she continued to listen to Deborah, she heard only half the words, so distracted was she by the Scotsman's physical presence.

She smiled at David and thanked him for bringing Miss Cohen, for she was enjoying her company.

"I had hoped you would like each other," David said. "Deborah, Mr. Gower would like to meet the other redhead in the room. Miss Deborah Cohen, Mr. Alec Gower."

"Did you suffer from childhood taunts, Miss Cohen?"

Deborah laughed. "I don't think I have ever gone through one day when someone hasn't commented on the color of my hair. Sometimes one feels one is only hair as a child."

"Aye, I know what you mean," said Alec.

"Or only tall," Barbara chimed in. "I always felt such a great gawk as a young girl. I was never allowed to forget my height."

"And I was always too dark," complained David, and they all laughed.

"It is painful to be different as a child, isn't it?" said Deborah. "One small thing, and you get teased unmercifully. I used to get into terrible fights," she continued without thinking, and looked around questioningly as everyone laughed again.

"It was not funny, I assure you. I would come home with my nose bloodied and my dress torn, and my mother was ready to despair."

"It is just that you are small, Deborah," said David.

"I gave as good as I got, I can assure you, David."

"Oh, I have no doubt about that," David replied, lowering his voice tenderly. Deborah blushed and was about to protest when Wardour wandered over to their little group.

"May I claim my fiancée?" he asked, and smoothly detached her from them, leaving Alec furious. He had had no time alone with Barbara, which was undoubtedly a good thing, but he resented Wardour's right to come in and break up their moments of good fellowship.

34

"I was right in the middle of a conversation, Peter," Barbara protested mildly.

"My mother tires easily, my dear, and wanted to spend some time with you before we leave. And I think it best you not spend too much time with Sir David and Miss Cohen."

Barbara had immediately worried about Lady Wardour feeling neglected as Wardour began. She was in front of his mother before she knew it and had no time to think of the import of Wardour's other remarks. But later that night she remembered them, and was determined to question him when he paid his next visit.

Wardour himself had been thinking about his brief comments, and wondered if they had been strong enough. He had no objection to Barbara having Sir David Treves as an acquaintance, but he obviously needed to make it clear to her that David could never be included as an intimate, either in town or at Arundel. Especially if he ended up marrying someone so obviously of his race as Miss Cohen.

He decided he would give Barbara a gentle warning the next time they were out in the park. He was surprised but relieved when Barbara herself brought the topic up on their next afternoon ride.

"Peter, the other night you made a comment about the amount of time I spent with Sir David and Miss Cohen."

"I am glad you brought this up, my dear, for I had intended to say a few more words to you this afternoon. I am sure you will agree with me when I say that it would be inappropriate for you to make close friends of either one of them."

"Inappropriate, Peter?" Barbara was determined to discover exactly where his objections came from. She suspected she knew, but didn't want to assume anything.

"Oh, I do not at all question your inviting them for a musical evening. I am liberal enough not to object to you numbering people like that among your acquaintances. But it would not be at all the thing to show them any special attention."

Barbara was beginning to get angry. She had never had anyone question either her choice of friends or the amount of time she spent with them. Even if Wardour was her fiancé, she deeply resented the implication that he could exercise any control over her actions. But she kept her voice under control.

"I am not sure what you mean by 'people like that,' Peter. People who enjoy music as I do?"

"Now, Barbara, I know that your family has a long tradition of radicalism . . ."

"Hardly radicalism, Peter," Barbara said dryly.

"Well, the Stanleys are Whig and the Wardours are Tory. But even you could not be so naive as to think it appropriate to cultivate an intimacy with people of another faith."

"You mean Jews, Peter."

"Actually, yes. Yes, I do," admitted Wardour, uncomfortable at having to spell it out.

"Then you should say what you mean. You believe that Sir David and I should not enjoy each other's company despite what we have in common merely because he is Jewish?"

"I am sure Sir David is an intelligent, cultivated man. But Barbara, surely you see that it is impossible."

"I don't think I do see, Peter. You must explain yourself better."

"I don't want to say anything offensive about Sir David, Barbara. He is, perhaps, an exception. But Jews are different from the rest of us. It doesn't matter that many of them can sound English. They are not and never can be. They think differently."

"Indeed, I suspect they do, and perhaps much better than you are thinking right now. I never realized this was something you felt so strongly about."

"Nor I," admitted Wardour. "There has never been a reason before for me to express my feelings on the subject. Oh, we have the occasional Jewish peddler in Arundel, trying to cheat the local farmers' wives, but there has never been any danger before now that a Jew would have anything to do with my family. Sir David would not be welcome in my home, Barbara," Wardour said, as gently as he could. "I just wanted to make that clear to you, to spare us any future embarrassment."

"You have made yourself quite clear, Peter," replied Barbara. She didn't know what made her angrier: that Wardour assumed he could control her choice of friends, or the reasons behind his desire to do so. She only knew that if she said anything further to him now, she was afraid she would regret it later. "I would like to return home now, Peter."

"We have only just got here, Barbara."

"I have the headache. I am rather tired from playing last night."

"Of course." Wardour signaled his groom to turn the horses. "I hope you understand I have spoken out of concern, my dear. I don't want any misunderstandings between us, or any awkwardness."

"You have made yourself clear, Peter, and I appreciate your motive." Robin would have been able to tell from Barbara's tight-lipped expression and the rigidity of her shoulders that she was very angry. Wardour, happily, had had no experience with controlled fury, and thought her reserve on the drive home was the result of her headache. He was solicitous as he escorted her to the door, and implored her to get some rest. "And if your headache is not gone before supper," he added, "do not hesitate to cancel our theater engagement."

35

Barbara wished she had had a real headache to distract her from the problem at hand. She was ashamed that her anger wasn't only at Wardour's intolerance, but also because he assumed his desires and preferences would naturally take precedence over hers. She had never thought of him as truly arrogant, and perhaps she was being unjust now. Was it arrogance to assume that a husband would have the final word? After all, most husbands she knew assumed their opinions were more important, and indeed, in law, their superiority was confirmed.

But his assumption of superiority was at least something they could have argued about and perhaps achieved a compromise on. His intolerance made her feel sick to her stomach. It so appalled her, coming from one she liked and respected, that she had felt paralyzed by it. What could one say to a man one thought one loved? Wardour was, after all, a good man. He loved his mother. He was generous to his sister. He was responsible and compassionate to those dependent upon him. And yet he disliked, nay, despised, she would guess, individual people for belonging to a particular religion.

Barbara felt as though she had been handed a beautiful red apple, which appeared perfect on the outside, and was indeed firm and juicy on the inside except for one small rotten spot near the core. But that one small black spot could corrupt the whole piece of fruit, and ultimately a whole basketful.

She could imagine herself fighting for more equality in her marriage. But could she imagine living with corruption, however little it would impinge directly on their lives? Yet David was a relatively new friend, not like Judith or Simon. She would feel sorry at his loss, she would mourn their companionship, but was losing his close friendship reason enough for breaking her engagement?

But what if Judith had been Jewish? Wardour would not have allowed her at Arundel. And what of their children? Did she want her children developing the same subtle prejudices their father held? Or their mother's complicity in them?

And what of those children? If she didn't marry Wardour, she would be unlikely to have them at all. She would be back to the limbo of the last six years. Wardour was likely to be her last chance at happiness and a home of her own. Was it worth it to turn it all down just for the sake of two acquaintances? She had come to feel a great affection for Peter; she was very attracted to him. Why should she give up the chance of their developing a passionate love for some quixotic notions about justice and equality? Robin had made a happy life with Diana, who had her share of intolerance.

She tried to dismiss David's importance in her life. But then she remembered clearly their first conversation and her feeling that she had discovered a spirit akin to her own. He was a rare friend, however new. Was she really willing to lose him?

Then, in one moment, for no reason Barbara could name, it all became clear. How could she ever contract a marriage which implicitly tolerated prejudice? She could imagine living with Peter easily enough. She could just not imagine living with herself. If she married Peter, she would be collaborating in the loss of her own integrity. And for better or worse, it was herself she had to live with, until death did them part.

Although she knew that sadness and the familiar loneliness would soon return, for the moment she felt a sort of peace and wholeness. No one would understand her decision. And she could tell no one her real reason for breaking the engagement, for it would be unfair to Wardour and incomprehensible to most of the *ton*. She would have to learn to live with the fact that people would gossip and invent reasons. And learn to live as spinster aunt and godmother, enjoying other people's children and never her own.

Barbara sent a short note to Wardour excusing herself from the theater because of her headache and asking him to call on her early in the morning.

She was so nervous she had only a cup of tea for breakfast. For the first time in months, she turned to music for comfort and informed the butler she would be in the music room. The Bach fugue she chose was demanding enough that all her concentration had to be focused on the intricacy of the music and not her personal worries. By the time Peter was announced, she was calm and prepared.

He had been shown into the drawing room and was paging through the *Post* when Barbara walked in.

"Good morning, Peter."

He stood up and quickly went to her, taking her hands in his. "I hope you are not still unwell, my dear. I worried about you all last night."

There was such genuine care and concern in his voice that Barbara almost doubted her decision. Peter loved her. Why on earth was she throwing that kind of devotion away? She so wanted to be loved.

But she also wanted to be able to love back, without reservation, she reminded herself. And she could not now give Peter the passionate response he deserved.

"I am perfectly recovered, thank you, Peter."

Wardour smiled and drew her into his arms for a kiss. Barbara held herself very still, and when he sensed the lack of her customary response, he lifted his head and looked at her questioningly. Barbara put her hands on his shoulders and gently pushed him away.

"Peter, I have something I need to tell you."

"Yes?" Wardour looked puzzled, as well he might. He had no real reason to think there were any difficulties between them.

She twisted her hands together nervously. "I have decided I cannot marry you, Peter."

"You have decided what?" he asked, as if he had not heard her correctly.

"Come, let us sit down," said Barbara, motioning him to the sofa and taking a chair opposite him. "I know this is unexpected. It is so for me also."

"I am sure I must be dreaming," said Wardour with an attempt at humor. "Surely you cannot have said what I thought you did. There is no possible reason for it."

"Perhaps you will not understand my reason, Peter. I realized two things last night. One, that I could not accept my husband dictating to me about my friends."

"You must know, Barbara, that I am no tyrant," protested Wardour. "Of course you may choose your friends freely. Under any other circumstances the topic would not have even arisen. But this is a unique situation."

"And that is the second and most important reason, Peter. Oh, I know there are bound to be conflicts in any marriage, and I would not want a husband who would let me run over him. And I suspected that if I protested, under different circumstances you would have given in to my wishes. Unfortunately, it is the circumstances that are the issue. One of my friends is Jewish, and because of that fact and that fact alone, you wish me to end the friendship."

"Now, Barbara," said Wardour in a reasonable tone, "I know our families' politics differ, but I am sure that on this question, they would be in agreement. It is one thing to include a person in a general invitation occasionally. I have no objection to that, I hasten to tell you. But a particular intimacy is out of the question. Surely you can see that."

"But that is just what I do not see, Peter. It is all right to accept money for Wellington's campaign from David's family, but it is not all right to be his friend? He is an intelligent, warm, amusing person, and one who shares my love for music. And, moreover, one who understands what it is like to be frustrated in one's deepest desires."

"I do not deny that Treves is intelligent and good company, my dear. That is not the point. The point is that Jews are different. They are not quite . . . English, and never will be. This is not something to argue about . . . I mean, I would assume that everyone would just take it for granted. And in what desire are you frustrated, Barbara? I thought our companionship to be everything either of us would want."

"Oh, Peter, it is *because* you take it for granted that I cannot marry you. Your intolerance is so ingrained in you that you cannot even question it. And although you are trying very hard to understand me, you really don't know what I am talking about. I could not bear seeing our children growing up with the same unquestioning prejudices."

"And our own relationship? How is that lacking?"

"It has made me very happy, Peter. I respect you in every other way and have a great affection for you. No, the desire I was talking about was music."

"But I would never dream of discouraging your music, Barbara."

"Oh, I know that. But neither do you comprehend how difficult it is to have talent and not be able to celebrate it."

"And Treves understands this?" Wardour asked, disbelief in his voice.

"David would have liked to study law, but it is a profession closed to him as a Jew."

"Of course. It makes sense for them to confine themselves to areas where their financial acumen is most useful. Just as it makes sense for women to confine themselves to home and children. You surely would not have wanted to traipse across the concert stages of Europe?"

"I don't know. But I will never have the opportunity to

find out, will I? I only know that it is very painful always to be holding myself back when I play with others."

"You did not hold yourself back the other night, my dear. And I am proud of your talent, Barbara."

"The other night was different," agreed Barbara, with a note in her voice that Wardour had never heard before. "And I do know that you appreciate me, Peter. But I still cannot marry you."

Wardour stood up, icily furious. "I think you are making the biggest mistake of your life, Lady Barbara. But if you so wish, I will release you from our engagement and do what I can to discourage any gossip."

"That is most kind of you, Peter." Barbara's eyes filled suddenly and she stood up and put out her hand. "This is not an easy or happy decision for me, you must know. I was looking forward to being your wife, Peter. I was very happy at Arundel."

"So you seemed to be," he answered coolly. "Well, good day, my dear. I hope you do not live to regret your decision." Wardour turned on his heel and went out the door, leaving Barbara with mixed feelings. She had wounded a kind, considerate man, who cared for her, and that she regretted. On the other hand, she found herself wondering if she had wounded his pride as much as his heart. She would never discover now whether all the elements in their relationship would have combined and produced a passionate marriage. She was also a little relieved that she didn't have to quiet that small voice anymore, which kept telling her that something was missing.

She sat down abruptly, suddenly exhausted by all of it: the attempt to explain the inexplicable to Wardour, the growing realization that she had probably turned away her only chance at marriage, and the underlying sadness that made itself felt whenever she thought about playing with Alec Gower. She kept trying to tell herself that it was an illusion that their deepest selves had come together. Great music can do that, make one feel one with everything, she told herself. But she had to admit that when she thought of Alec, she did not only think of his rare talent or the meeting of their souls. What also came to mind was the memory of his fine strong legs and twinkling blue eyes and the joy that had bubbled up on their first meeting.

I must be the world's greatest fool, Barbara thought. Oh, how I wish Judith were here!

36

Within a few days the word was out that the engagement between Lady Barbara Stanley and the Marquess of Wardour was at an end. Wardour, true to his word, answered all questions by saying that he and Lady Barbara had mutually decided that they would not suit. He stayed in London for over a week, when he would have preferred to return immediately to Arundel, and when he and Barbara were at the same social gatherings, he made sure to be seen with her, and even, upon occasion, asked her to dance.

It was a painful time for both of them. Barbara made a separate call on Lady Wardour to bid her farewell, and both had tears in their eyes by the time the visit was over. Although Robin understood the grounds of her decision, Diana thought she was being foolishly idealistic. "After all, Barbara," she said to her sister-in-law over breakfast one morning, "Wardour's request was not at all unreasonable. I have myself wondered at your growing intimacy with Sir David. I know that Robin does not agree with me, but it is one thing for men to get together over politics and quite another to make someone a part of your intimate circle."

Robin broke in gently but firmly. "Diana, you and I have come to an understanding on this. But as your husband, I could impose my choices on you if I so wished. I don't," Robin continued, as Diana began to protest that he had never been that unreasonable. "But Barbara would have been entering a marriage where she would have had to give up a good friend for reasons that were untenable for her."

"I still say that Wardour was not being at all unreasonable. Not that I don't like Sir David. I do. But . . ."

"He is a Jew," continued Barbara quietly.

"Well, yes," Diana admitted.

"Diana, I respect the way you and Robin have managed to allow each other the freedom to disagree. But, as you have said, Robin has never dictated to you who your friends should be. I could not have lived with it."

"Well, when you put it like that, I understand a little better. I would not take well to domestic tyranny myself," Diana admitted.

"I don't even perceive Peter as a tyrant," said Barbara. "I think he is just used to getting his own way."

"You must admit that he has been every bit a gentleman about it."

"He has indeed," Barbara replied.

"Well, I hope Sir David appreciates your sacrifice, Barbara."

"I have only told him that we had discovered an irreconcilable difference between us. And as I did it for myself, not for him, he need know nothing more."

When Wardour finally left for Kent, Barbara felt a little sadness combined with great relief. It had been difficult to be in public with him. He was always polite, but cool and reserved. She had wondered if he would seek some private conversation with her to persuade her to change her mind, but they had never been alone together, and from what she could see, he had no desire to say anything to her above the commonplace. She was glad not to be pressured, but a bit hurt that he could let her go so easily.

David had acted the good friend: not intrusive, but always available as an escort when she needed one. They continued their morning rides, and after his first attempts to convey his sympathy, he took Barbara's cue and kept away from the subject altogether.

The Little Season was drawing to a close, and on one of

their rides David wondered aloud what Alec Gower was going to do for employment once the *ton* left town. "I suppose he could find a position as a music teacher," mused David.

"Mr. Gower seems very resilient to me, David. I am sure he will find something." Barbara did not want to talk about the Scotsman. She did not want to think about him or begin to wonder where he was going next.

"I would have to agree with you. He is an interesting combination, our Mr. Gower, isn't he, of busker and classical musician? He can switch so easily from broad Scots to perfect English. I have always wondered what his background is."

"He could be anything, couldn't he? What is most likely is that he comes from a good background, but decided he wanted music more than a position in the family business or becoming some nobleman's secretary."

"You are probably right. He is a puzzle," said David with a smile. "But a most talented and amusing one."

37

The talented and amusing puzzle in question was at that moment going through his belongings as he prepared for his return to Scotland. He should have been feeling triumphant: he had won his wager, or at least would have by the time he returned home. His grandfather would not be happy, but was a man of his word, so Alec would be free to pursue his music. He was certainly happy about that—but then, he had known from the beginning that he could win this wager. What took away from his victory was the tremendous sadness he felt at leaving Lady Barbara. She would be Lady Wardour by the time he returned to London in the spring, and there was nothing he could do about it. He had ten days left of being Alec Gower, and if he revealed himself, he forfeited his whole life. And even if he did speak, what could he say to her? "Don't marry Wardour. I love you. And by the way, I am not an itinerant musician, but the grandson of a duke." Whatever the feelings that had flowed between them when they played, Barbara seemed to be happy in her engagement and he had no right to disturb that.

The next day, before he left, Alec returned to Treves and Son to bid David farewell.

"I am back to Scotland, David, but I wanted to thank you again for your help and bid you good-bye."

"I did very little, Alec. Your own music is what insured your engagements."

"Could you do a favor for me?"

"Of course."

"Could you thank Lady Barbara Stanley . . . or perhaps she is already Lady Wardour . . . for her recommending me to you?"

"You haven't heard? She has broken her engagement to Wardour. And I will convey your message to her."

Alec was too astonished by the news not to express his disbelief. "I am truly surprised. When I was at Arundel this summer, it seemed as though all was going very well between them."

"I don't quite understand it myself," admitted David. "And I have not pressed Barbara for a fuller explanation. But I must say that I never liked Wardour that much. I have always thought she needed someone more appreciative of her talent."

"Wardour seemed very proud of her."

"Oh, he would like to show off his talented wife, I am sure. He would think it no more than he deserved. No, I meant more that she needs someone more like yourself, who understands her passion for music."

Alec said his good-byes quickly and found himself out on the street wanting to do a wild Highland fling. He allowed himself one side kick, to the great amusement of passers-by, before he hurried off to collect his things. If Barbara was not to marry Wardour, then there was some hope for him. He was anxious to reach Scotland as quickly as possible, and after counting his money, decided he could afford to take the stage as long as he was willing to play for his suppers.

David had watched him go and laughed at the sight of him kicking up his heels. What would have been funny in pantaloons was even more amusing with a kilt swinging out behind. He wondered what had brought on that small explosion of joie de vivre. Was Gower that happy to go home?

As he turned back to his work, he realized that he had spoken the truth. Barbara did need someone just like Gower, and what a pity it was that he was inappropriate.

38

The Stanleys left town a few days later. Barbara was happy to be home, where the only socializing to be done was with well-loved neighbors. No one mentioned the broken engagement except the vicar's wife, who expressed her sympathy in such a considerate way that Barbara was not at all uncomfortable. She knew, of course, that people were gossiping, but country gossip at Ashurst didn't bother her. Most of the people cared for her, and those who didn't she had dismissed as unimportant long ago.

She rode as often as she could, although the ground was getting harder as cold weather set in. She found herself often riding by the copse where Alec Gower had camped, and instead of bare trees, saw sunlight and green leaves and a merry face smiling up at her.

The one good thing that had happened after the broken engagement was that music again become her consolation. She threw herself into practicing every morning, and succeeded for the most part at keeping memory at bay. She never played Mozart, for fear that even a measure of his music might bring back that particular sonata.

Judith had completely recovered, and Barbara was looking forward to the holidays, when the Suttons were planning to come for a week's visit. She had also invited David, but he had written to excuse himself, explaining that he wanted to rediscover his own festival of light with Miss Cohen.

In early December the weather turned very cold. It

snowed several times before Christmas and Barbara was
worried that Judith and her family would not be able to
travel. There was a thaw, however, a few days before
Christmas, and so the Suttons arrived safely.

Baby Robin looked almost chubby, having begun to
catch up with himself, and Judith was blooming. Sophy al-
ternated between proudly holding her baby brother and then
planting kisses on him that seemed designed to smother
him. After one particularly vehement kiss, the baby started
to howl. When Judith told her daughter that she must remember to be gentle with her baby brother, Sophy's lower
lip began to tremble, and she turned and clung to her father's legs.

"I am afraid having two children around is a very different proposition than one," said Judith.

"Don't worry," said Robin with a grin, as Sophy was
borne away by her nurse. "We are used to it."

"I only hope the holiday isn't ruined."

As it turned out, having other children around as well as
several adults who doted on her greatly relieved Sophy's
jealousy, and so the week was peaceful after all.

One afternoon after Christmas, when Sophy was playing
with the twins and the baby sleeping soundly, Judith and
Barbara found the time for a quiet coze.

"You don't look happy, Barbara. Are you suffering from
any regrets about Wardour?" asked Judith, concerned about
her friend.

"No, not really, Judith. As I told you in my letter, I could
not have been happy under those circumstances. It is just
that I feel I turned down my last chance for a home and
family of my own."

"I hardly think so," protested Judith. "You are barely
twenty-six!"

"And decidedly on the shelf."

"Look at Nora. She found Sam even later in life. It is
never too late for love, Barbara."

"But Nora had a child to keep her company. I hope I can

keep myself from becoming an eccentric or embittered old spinster aunt."

"You do have your music."

"Yes, and I am finding comfort in it again. Although, at times, it reminds me of someone I would wish not to remember," she added, almost to herself.

"Mr. Gower?"

"Yes," Barbara replied, looking shamefaced.

"I am sure that your feeling for Mr. Gower will fade away, and I predict that within a year you will have met someone who makes you forget everyone else."

"Oh, and are you going to take the fortune-teller's place at the Midsummer Fair this year, Madame Judith?" teased Barbara.

"Perhaps I will." Judith laughed. "For I feel, in the oddest way, quite sure that I am right."

Barbara laughed at herself many times over the next weeks. For some reason, absurd as it might seem, Judith's confidence in her prediction gave her hope, and it was only that hope that got her through the lonely winter.

39

Alec had reached Strathyre well before the holidays. He went straight to his parents' home, where he was greeted as a long-lost sheep by his mother. He received a more subdued welcome from his father, who looked with distaste at his ragged kilt and dirty plaid.

Alec tossed a shilling onto the hall table. "There . . . you are both witness to the fact that I came home with silver in my pocket."

"You are determined to pursue this foolish course?" asked his father.

"I didna sleep in haymows and barns and freeze ma ar— knees off, Father, on a whim. Yes, I intend to go to London in the spring."

"Ah, dinna talk of leaving again, Alec dearie," said his mother, giving him a desperate hug.

"Why the two of you persist in that vulgar tongue, I'll never know," said his father, not for the first time.

"'Tis the language of my home and heart, as well you know, George," answered his wife in perfectly accented English. "And 'twas one of the things you fell in love with me for, or so you told me then."

"Aha, that's a story I've never heard before," said Alec.

"Enough, the two of you," said his father. "Your grandfather will be expecting you tonight, Alec. You'd better bathe and shave and change, my boy. It is good to have you home." He extended his hand and Alec grabbed it and pulled his father into a hearty hug.

He was more subdued when he went to call on the duke. His hair was trimmed, his beard gone, and he was impeccably dressed in a maroon coat and fawn breeches.

When he was admitted to the library, he couldn't help smiling with delight, however. He loved the old man despite their disagreements and was genuinely glad to see him.

"I understand you have come to gloat," said the duke, having successfully kept all expressions of happiness at the prodigal's return from his face.

"Not at all, Grandfather," protested Alec. "I am simply glad to see you."

"Sit down, sit down. It makes me uncomfortable looking up at you."

This time Alec avoided the sofa and pulled up a chair.

"So I am to understand that you made your way solely by your music?"

"I did, my lord."

"You never used your name to gain anything?"

"Never, Grandfather. Although at the end I was sorely tempted."

"Aha . . . you were running out of funds?"

"No, not at all. No, the truth is, I met a woman . . ."

"Hmmmph. What kind of woman could you have met while wandering the highways?"

"Perhaps I should have said I met a lady," replied Alec dryly.

"A lady?"

"Lady Barbara Stanley."

"Stanley . . . Stanley? Not the Stanleys of Norfolk?"

"No."

"Good. A bunch of rakehell men and dim-witted women, from what I know."

"The Earl of Ashurst's daughter."

"Ashurst, eh. Never very political. Nice enough fellow, bright enough. Just always racketing about with that wife of his. More than one child, wasn't there?"

"Lady Barbara has a brother, Major Robert Stanley."

"Ah, yes. One of Wellington's men. I met him once, I think. A little too Whiggish for my taste. What of this Lady Barbara? You could hardly have been socializing with her."

"I met her at their Midsummer Fair and then later at her fiancé's house, where we had the opportunity to play together."

"Play together?"

"She is a fine pianist, Grandfather. I was hired as a musician and she joined me on one piece."

"She is betrothed to someone else. I hope she is not one of those women who dallies with the lower classes."

Alec flushed with anger. "Barbara is a lady not just in name, my lord. Our relationship never went beyond proper bounds."

"Well, it sounds as if you resisted temptation, which is all to the good, since she is betrothed."

"I did resist, for her sake and mine. But just before I left London, I heard her engagement had been broken."

"Who broke it off?"

"I don't know, my lord, neither do I care. But I am looking forward to wooing her in the spring."

"So you intend to pursue music?"

"I did win our wager, Grandfather."

"And I am a man of my word, as well you know."

"Thank you. I will return to London in the early spring. As I told you, I will be studying and composing for the most part. But if the opportunity to perform arises, I may take advantage of it infrequently."

"Just so long as you do not turn yourself into a hired musician again."

"With Grandmother's legacy, I will hardly have to do that," said Alec with a grateful smile.

"Do you think you have a chance with this Lady Barbara? Could she be interested in the eccentric grandson of a duke who persists in a wholly unsuitable career?"

"I don't know, my lord, but I assure you, I fully intend to find out."

40

Alec spent a comfortable winter with his family, but as the spring approached he became more and more restless. He made up his mind to leave Scotland as soon as the roads were clear. Accordingly, in early March, he was ready to leave for London to find permanent lodgings.

"We will be opening the town house this Season, Alec. You know you are welcome there," said his mother.

"I know, Mother. But I need peace and quiet to play and to write. It is time I had my own rooms."

"You will take part in the Season, won't you?"

"Yes, this time you have me, my dear."

"You don't fool me, Alec. You will be there for Lady Barbara, not for your family."

"Now, Mother, you have not socialized much with the Sassenach yourself these past years."

"I know. It is your grandfather who prefers London to Edinburgh, not us. Take good care of yourself, my dear."

"I will, Mother. And I look forward to seeing you in April."

When he arrived in town, Alec went straight to Fenton's and reserved rooms for a week, while he sought out more permanent lodgings. After three days of searching and finding nothing suitable, he decided to enlist David Treves' help. He had liked David instantly and was sure the feeling had been mutual, despite the difference in their social positions. And as a young man on the fringes of the *ton*, Treves should be able to direct him to the sort of neighborhood he wanted: not Mayfair, but not too unfashionable.

When he arrived at Treves and Son, he announced himself as Mr. Gower. This time the clerk was suitably obsequious, not because he remembered him, but because Alec was dressed impeccably. When David emerged from the back with a smile on his face, Alec was glad he had come, for he was sure there was potential for a firm friendship.

"Alec! What a surprise," said David, taking in every inch of the fashionable gentleman in front of him.

"I can tell by your face it is my appearance as well as my presence that startles you, David," replied Alec in his most cultured tones.

"You must admit that a Weston coat is a bit different from your plaid, Alec. That is a Weston, if I am not mistaken?"

"I have something to confess to you, David."

"Well, let's not make it public. Come back to my office. I have some sherry there and we can celebrate your reappearance."

Once they were seated and drinking, David looked at Alec and asked in semiserious tones whether he had seduced an heiress or had had a particularly good winter busking. "Or did you rob the mail coach? Come, come, it is time to confess."

"Och, it is worse than that, Davie," said Alec, rolling his *r*'s. "I am afraid I hae deceived ye."

"Aha, you are the son of a Scottish baron and couldn't reveal yourself for some mad reason," said David with a laugh.

"Close, Davie, close. But it is worse than that. I am the grandson of a duke and the second son of a marquess. My name is not Alec Gower. I am Lord Alexander MacLeod, at your service," answered his friend with a mock bow.

"You're bamming me!"

"I am not."

"Then why, by all that's holy, were you traipsing around as an itinerant musician?"

"Because that is what I was last year. You see, my grandfather cannot endure the idea of a MacLeod making a career of music. I had a wager with him: if I could make my way for a year just with my fiddle and without making use of the family name, then he would release my inheritance and allow me to choose musical composition over legal depositions," Alec explained with a flourish of his hand.

"And you won."

"I won. Thanks, in part, to you, my friend. I hope I can count you as a friend?" asked Alec. "Here I have been calling you Davie . . ."

"I liked you from the start, Alec. But are you sure you wish to count me amongst your friends?"

"Whyever not? Oh, the Jewish question." Alec dismissed that with another wave of his hand. "Och, Davie, we maun hold togither against the Sassenach."

"What of your grandfather?"

"A Scotsman too, though he would like to forget it and act like one of them."

"A common story."

"Aye, We both know how to balance two identities, don't we?"

"Where are you staying?" David asked.

"Now, that is why I came to see you. I am putting up at Fenton's, but am looking for rooms. I thought you might know of a place appropriate for a musician."

"As a matter of fact, I know just the place. You can have my rooms. I am moving out in a fortnight."

"Not out of London, I hope?"

"No, I am getting married," David announced, his face flushed with both pride and embarrassment.

"To that splendid redhead who was with you at the Stanleys'?"

"Yes, to Miss Deborah Cohen. We have purchased a house."

"I wish you very happy, Davie," Alec said, lifting his glass. "How *is* Lady Barbara by the way?"

He tried to sound matter-of-fact, and seemed to have succeeded, for David answered as though it were just normal curiosity that prompted the question.

"She spent the winter in Sussex, of course. Wardour was quite the gentleman about the whole thing, so that most of the gossip had died down before the holidays. I expect she will be in town within the week. She is, of course, invited to the wedding." David opened his mouth as though he were going to continue and then closed it again.

"You were about to say something?"

"Well, the thought had occurred to me . . . umm . . . I was just going to wonder aloud about Barbara's reaction to your real identity. I was also thinking that the two of you would make a natural couple. Forgive me, but my approaching nuptials have turned me into a matchmaker."

"I am sure the lady has many admirers."

"Oh, yes, but Wardour was the only one she had ever encouraged."

"Do you think she is still wearing the willow?"

David looked thoughtful. "I might be wildly off the mark, but when I conveyed my sympathy to Barbara in the fall, she seemed to be suffering more from a general disappointment than a particular heartache. She told me that they had mutually agreed that they would not suit."

"I am relieved to hear that, for I fully intend to woo her this spring."

"So I am not being foolishly romantic," David said with a wide smile.

"Och, Davie, we may both be foolish. Who knows how the lady will react to me? For all I know, she has forgotten Alec Gower and I will have to start all over again."

41

Madame Judith's prediction might have gotten Barbara through the winter at Ashurst, but the approach of the Season brought her back to the hard facts of her spinsterhood. She would be returning for her seventh Season and, she was determined, her last. After this Spring, she would retire gracefully, start wearing a cap, and resign herself to her fate. The only reason she had even agreed to accompany Robin and Diana to London was for appearances' sake. If she stayed at Ashurst, the gossips would be sure to notice and comment again on her broken engagement. She would have to hide her boredom and loneliness under a carefree facade to earn the retirement from society that she desired. She could only hope that Wardour had decided to stay at Arundel this spring. She did not think she had the courage to face him again and pretend to be good friends.

It was a surprise, therefore, to hear almost immediately after they arrived in London that not only was Wardour in Kent, but newly married to the youngest daughter of his neighbor, the Viscount Fulcomb. Barbara remembered her as a very pretty girl who had shyly complimented Barbara on her music. "But she is barely eighteen," she protested, when Robin gently broke the news.

"Are you terribly upset?" he asked.

"If you mean, do I have any regrets, Robin, no, not at all. But I must confess to more than a little wounded vanity. After all, his new wife is almost a decade younger than I! I feel like Methusaleh. I am relieved, however, to hear that he recovered so quickly," continued Barbara tartly. "And I suspect his new bride will be much more suitable and pliant than I. I wish him happy, I truly do."

"And I wish you the same happiness, Barbara. Perhaps this Season . . ."

"Judith has great hopes for this spring," Barbara replied with patently false gaiety. "Perhaps she is right and I'll see some old acquaintance with new eyes. Stranger things have happened."

But old acquaintances looked the same, thought Barbara a few days into the Season, as she surveyed the crush at the Rosses' ball. Her dance card was almost full, but as she read it over she realized that she had danced with these same men year after year. She knew whose feet would tread on her slippers, whose hand would squeeze her waist during the waltz, and who would compliment her, yet again, on the way her gown matched her eyes. Thank God David was down for a waltz, she thought.

When, a few minutes later, she heard David announced, along with Lord Alexander MacLeod, she looked around eagerly for his tall, dark-haired figure. When she saw him, she smiled naturally for the first time that night and began to make her way through the crowd. As she got closer, however, her smile disappeared, for standing with his back toward her was a tall, auburn-haired stranger, who reminded her so strongly of Alec Gower that her knees felt weak. Oh, why did someone with the same color hair, the same broad shoulders, have to be here tonight? She thought she had cured herself of her foolishness, but apparently not, if merely the sight of dark-red hair undid her. Had David not seen her and smiled at her, she would have broken and run.

She focused on David, refusing to glance to her right. She had to turn at last, as David introduced her to Lord Alexander MacLeod, and found herself looking into the bright blue eyes of Alec Gower. What had David called him? She offered her hand and opened her mouth, but was struck dumb by the surprise, and stood there gaping like a fish.

"I was as surprised as you are," David said, coming to her rescue. "Alec told me his story, however, which explains his disguise."

"Indeed?" said Barbara, finally finding her voice.

"I told David about a certain wager," started Alec.

"Wager? Was your deception the result of some drunken night out, then?" asked Barbara in her chilliest tones. "How interesting and how commonplace," she added dismissively. "Excuse me, gentlemen, but I see Lady Vane over there and wish to coax her into talking about her new grandchild." Barbara was gone before Alec or David could say a word.

"Well, hardly what I'd call an auspicious beginning to my wooing, Davie," said Alec.

"I think I would have to agree with you," said David, smiling despite himself. "But it was a shock to be introduced to you like that, with no warning."

"Aye, but there was no better way to do it. It is done now, for better or worse. For worse, it would seem," admitted Alec with a wry grin.

"Now, don't give up hope. I will make sure you have some time with her tonight."

Talking to Nora about her new granddaughter was not difficult, for she was ecstatic about little Margaret Lavinia. By the time her husband, accompanied by David, joined them, Barbara had recovered from her shock and let David confirm his two dances before she was swept off by her next partner.

When the time came for David to claim his waltz, he was nowhere to be seen, and Barbara was about to sit down when Alec Gower—no, Lord Alexander—appeared before her.

"Sir David is unavoidably detained, and begged me to take his place," Alec announced.

"David, I suspect, has hidden in some corner and sent you over instead, Mr. Gower. I mean Lord Alexander."

Alec's eyes twinkled down at her. "You're a canny lassie, but will ye no dance wi' me all the same? Unless you are too tired," he added, in his best English. "In that case, perhaps we could find a private corner for conversation."

"No, I am not quite at my last prayers, my lord," replied Barbara. Surely dancing would be easier than a private chat, but she shivered uncontrollably when Alec put his arm around her.

"You are cold, Lady Barbara?" he asked, with such a concern in his voice that she almost lost her composure.

"Just a goose walking over my grave," she said lightly, trying to ignore the warmth of his arm around her waist and the feeling of her hand in his.

Alec had no desire to ruin the dance with explanations, so he kept silent. Barbara would have expected their silence to be strained and uncomfortable, but the longer they danced, the more relaxed she felt. They danced as they had played, effortlessly, and by the time the music stopped, she was only sorry that their closeness must end.

"I would like to talk to you, Lady Barbara," said Alec seriously. "I believe I owe you an explanation. May we go out on the balcony for some privacy?"

Barbara was too bewitched to refuse, and they slipped out through the French doors and faced one another, breathless from their waltz and the realization that the next few minutes could determine the course of their acquaintance.

"I am not given to drunken wagers, Lady Barbara, and I want you to know that," Alec began. "There were unique circumstances, as I think you will agree." And he explained the whole. "So you see, it was absolutely necessary that I not reveal myself to anyone, even when I wished to."

"And you assure me that 'Alec Gower' was the disguise, and not 'Lord Alexander,'" she said, only half teasing.

"Oh, aye. My parents and my grandfather are just arrived and I know that you will be meeting them at some party or other. Will that convince you?"

"Oh, I am convinced, my lord. In fact, I always wondered about Mr. Gower and how he could play Mozart as well as he could a reel. I suspected you were from some good family, although not of the nobility, I admit. And so you will be able to make your dream come true," she added wistfully. "It is easier for a man, even if he is the grandson of an earl."

"Up to a point. I will be free to study and compose. Perhaps get away with a public performance occasionally. But most of my playing will be for friends and family, as yours is. My father and grandfather are in good health and have long lives ahead of them, as does my brother, I hope. But one never knows, which is why I was so determined to have this time now."

"I wish you well, my lord," said Barbara.

"I was hoping . . . that is . . . would it be possible for us to play together again? If you have forgiven me for my deception."

"There is little to forgive, my lord. After all, your masquerade harmed no one. Perhaps we could look forward to a duet again."

"I have a sonata of my own composition, for fortepiano and violin. I would love to practice it with you." Alec did not add that he had spent the winter working on this piece with Barbara in mind.

"I would be free on Thursday," Barbara replied, shocking herself by her own boldness, but not wanting to let him go before they had set a date.

"Thursday it will be, then," agreed Alec.

42

The next few days went by very slowly, and Barbara found herself unable to concentrate on anything for longer than ten minutes. She would sit down to her music, begin her warm-up scales, play the first three measures, and then have to get up and move. Only a visit from David and Deborah to discuss their wedding plans was able to keep her attention focused for any length of time.

Deborah had insisted on being married from her home, a decision that had displeased the Treves family, which had wanted to make the wedding more of a social occasion than a religious ceremony.

"Deborah has been quite stubborn about this," said David.

"It is not stubbornness, David," Deborah started to protest.

"You can see that my fiancée's temper is as fiery as her hair," announced David in a loud aside to Barbara.

"It is quite untrue," protested Deborah, immediately incensed, "that redheaded people have a quicker temper than others."

"Yes, David," added Barbara, with a twinkle in her eye, "I am surprised at you for repeating that old saw when Miss Cohen is clearly the meekest of women."

Deborah blushed and then joined the others in their laughter.

"Perhaps there is a grain of truth in it after all," she admitted. "But I do not think it stubbornness to wish to be married from my own home. It will be hard enough to leave my father behind as it is."

David took her hand in his. "I promise you, you will be leaving no one behind, my dear. We will only be in another part of London, and you know I have the greatest liking for your father."

"I know, David," she replied. "I just find it difficult," she confessed to Barbara, "to go from poverty to riches so suddenly. I do not want to leave anything of my self behind. Nor am I ashamed of who I am. Which is why we will be married in the East End in a traditional wedding."

"And I am honored to be invited," said Barbara.

"We are very lucky to have family and good friends to be with us. Sarah will be the ring bearer."

"If she doesn't pocket it, my dear!"

"And Lord Alexander is to play for us."

"Lord Alexander will be there?" asked Barbara.

"We have become fast friends," David told her. "And it will be wonderful to have his music at our wedding."

"Well, I am looking forward to this. I think it will be the high point in a long, dull Season."

After they left, Barbara thought about how easily she might have given in to Wardour, and despite her loneliness, how happy she was to be free. Free to choose her own friends, free to attend their wedding. Free to dream of a certain Scotsman. . . .

How right David and Deborah were together. Deborah's fieriness was just what David needed, thought Barbara. Not only did her looks contrast wonderfully with his dark and melancholy handsomeness, but her strong sense of who she was had helped David out of ambivalence. While Barbara could well understand the desire to be fully accepted in society, she did not think that denying one's identity would make for ultimate happiness. She was glad that David had found Deborah and not gone along with his family's plans to have him marry into the nobility. Deborah was just the wife for him, and ultimately David would be happier fighting for acceptance politically than marrying his way in.

When Thursday arrived at last and Lord Alexander MacLeod was announced, Barbara had to take several deep breaths to calm herself before she entered the morning room.

Alec stood up immediately as she entered, and she took in every inch of him before she came forward. He was dressed in a forest-green coat and fawn pantaloons, and looked every inch the fashionable gentleman, yet Barbara found she missed his kilt. She banished her memory of his bare legs immediately, however, and welcoming him, asked if he wished some refreshment before they practiced.

"No, thank you, Lady Barbara," he answered rather stiffly. "I have less time this morning than I thought, so perhaps we should just begin."

Barbara felt a sharp stab of disappointment and cursed herself for her foolishness. The man was only here for music, she told herself. Heaven knows, he would not expect a lady to have been attracted to a busker. She led Alec to the music room and, seating herself immediately, waited for him to unpack his case.

"Here is the music, Lady Barbara," he said as he placed it in front of her. "Perhaps we could start with the second movement, since that is the most intricate."

"Of course. But you must be patient with me, my lord, for you know your own music well, and I am new to it."

The second movement was an allegro, and as they played it the first time, Barbara was concentrating so much on her reading that she could not fully enjoy it. But as they went through it again, she began to feel the music. Alec had managed to capture the spirit of a Scottish reel within a solidly classical form. The sonata was a sonata, but it was no clichéd imitation of a master. Instead, he had used the form to express a native *joie de vivre,* and Barbara felt again that pure joy welling up in her as she played. And yet, when they finished and she turned to face Alec, there were unshed tears in her eyes.

"Are you all right?" he asked.

"All right? Oh, these." She smiled, brushing her hand across her eyes. "Tears of joy, I think," she added tremulously. "You have written a wonderful allegro, my lord. I could almost hear Alec Gower's fiddle."

"You liked it?" he asked anxiously, forgetting his concern for her in his artist's insecurity.

"Like is a weak word for what I feel. You have revitalized the form, brought something new and original to it."

"Thank you, Lady Barbara, for recognizing what I attempted to do."

"You succeeded, my lord, I assure you."

"What do you think of this measure?" he asked, leaning forward to turn back a page. His hand brushed her cheek and she sat very still, willing him to stay there, close to her, his breath softly stirring her hair, as he sought his place. Did he linger on purpose? she wondered. Did he feel their closeness or was he only thinking of his music?

"Here. Can we play this again at a slower tempo?"

All business. "Of course, my lord." Why had she thought that if she was attracted to him, he must needs be to her?

They played the piece through once more, but this time Barbara was on guard against her emotions. She still felt delight, but did not let it carry her away. And so she was able to offer her hand and bid Alec good-bye quite calmly.

"Will I be seeing you at Heseltines's?"

"Yes, Robin and Diana and I have been invited."

"Until then," said Alec, and waved his good-bye.

"Till then," repeated Barbara, unsure of whether she was looking forward to or dreading their next meeting.

43

The Stanleys arrived early to the Heseltines's party, and Barbara saw no sign of Alec. She tried to appear interested in the conversation around her and willed herself not to turn her head each time the next guest was announced. She felt very foolish, for there had been nothing, after all, to indicate more than a friendly interest on Alec's part. He obviously saw her as a musical partner and nothing else.

When he was at last announced, she allowed herself to look across to the receiving line. He was accompanied by a tall woman with gray-streaked auburn hair who could only be his mother and two slender gentlemen, one with an abundance of silver hair. Alec towered over them, or so it seemed to her from that distance.

Before she could tell whether he had seen her and whether he intended to introduce her to his family, she was claimed for a country dance.

"Is the Lady Barbara Stanley here, Alec?" inquired the duke, who was gazing imperiously around.

Alec had seen Barbara immediately and had been about to approach her when she moved onto the dance floor.

"She is in the second set of the dance, Grandfather. The tall blond lassie who is stuck with the undersized and over-bellied guardsman."

"Alec!" chided his mother.

"Ah, well, Mother, but we danced so well together the other night that it fair makes me want to weep."

"Are you never serious, Alec?" asked his father.

"I promise you, I am very serious about this young woman."

When the music stopped, Alec was quick to approach Barbara and bring her over to his family.

"Lady Barbara Stanley, my grandfather, the Duke of Strathyre. My father, the Marquess of Doune. And Lady Doune."

"I am delighted to meet you all. You are not down for the Season often?"

Alec's mother smiled. "Not if we can help it. My father-in-law is in London frequently for political business, but we prefer to go only as far as Edinburgh."

The duke said nothing beyond his first greeting, but as others joined their little group, Barbara was always conscious of his presence. For a small man, he exuded an almost palpable sense of power. She glanced over occasionally, but could see nothing revealed on his face. She marveled that someone as open as Alec was a part of this family, but it became clear, during the next quarter hour, that he had inherited his mother's warmth and sense of humor.

"They are striking up a waltz, Lady Barbara. May I have the honor?" asked Alec.

"Why, yes, I believe I am free," answered Barbara, barely glancing at her dance card. To tell the truth, she did not care whether she had already promised the dance. She wanted to feel Alec's arm around her again.

They were silent for the first few measures, enjoying their compatibility once again. When Alec finally spoke, Barbara almost regretted his breaking the spell.

"What did you think of the MacLeod family, lassie?"

"I think your grandfather must be a formidable opponent, political or otherwise. Indeed, despite the fact that he and I are of a height, I felt he was looking down on me. I admire you for challenging him."

Alec chuckled. "Yes, I learned a long time ago that my

size gave me no advantage over either my father or the duke. In fact, when I was younger, it worked against me. I ever felt the clumsy oaf as an adolescent. It took me years to learn how to deal with them."

"And how is that?"

"With charm and guile, lassie. How else?"

"Not a thing to brag about," replied Barbara with tart humor, as the music came to an end and he guided her off the dance floor and over to the refreshment table.

"Ach, I learned a long time ago that you cannot go head to head with unbending power. You must flow over and around it. Like water over a rock."

"Or like quicksilver."

Alec smiled down at her. "Not quite so slippery as that, my lady. I am a very concentrated fellow when going after what I want."

"Yes, your success as a busker certainly proves that," admitted Barbara. "You wanted your music and you got it."

"And is there anything you want?" asked Alec.

"Oh, once I would have envied you your freedom to choose, but I think I am finally content with music's place in my life."

"Our lot is not all that different. I am not as constrained as a woman, but I am by rank. I am confined to composition rather than performance, as I have told you already. Although I have held onto the old plaid in case I get restless!" he added, his eyes twinkling. "But is there nothing else you want in life? You were betrothed last year. I do not mean to pry, but did you not lose something you wanted then?"

Barbara looked up in surprise and then quickly down, embarrassed by the concern in Alec's eyes. "I thought I wanted to be Wardour's wife. But then I came to know him better and decided we would not suit."

"He seemed a very kind and serious man to me."

"He was—is—a kind man. But there was an area of disagreement we discovered which made it impossible for me to marry him."

"It must have been something important to make you give up someone you loved," Alec said gently. He knew he was going beyond politeness, but he wanted to find out if she had any lingering regrets.

"Well, I am not at all sure now if I loved him. I suppose I didn't, if love is defined as giving up a piece of oneself."

"Was it your music, lass?"

"In part. He saw it as something analogous to sketching or embroidery, appropriate for a woman when not taken too seriously." Barbara hesitated and then decided to tell Alec the whole. "The heart of our disagreement was over whom I could choose as friends. He wished me to end my acquaintance with David Treves," said Barbara. "I found I could not do so."

Alec had known months ago that he wanted Barbara. That he was in love with her. But until now he had not known her except through music. He thought of the courage it had taken to give up an ideal marriage for a private moral conviction, and knew that he was lucky indeed to have fallen in love with a woman he could share more than music with. He had found someone he could also love.

Alec's silence worried Barbara.

"You think I was foolish, I suppose."

"Ah, lassie, would that the world had more fools like you," he said, and his hand caressed her cheek so quickly and so lightly that she could almost doubt he had touched her at all.

"David knows nothing of this and I do not wish him to," she said. "I did not do it for him, but for myself. Do you understand the difference?"

"I do, lass, I do. As a Scot, I have sometimes been on the receiving end of liberal gestures that humiliate more than offer friendship."

"Thank you for understanding. You are one of the few people who does."

Alec broke the tension of the moment by asking her what she thought of his "wee mither" and she laughed delightedly at the thought of Lady Doune, who was an inch taller than herself, being referred to as "wee."

They danced once more that evening, but their conversation returned to its light and humorous level. When they bade each other good-night, it was with the promise of seeing one another at David and Deborah's wedding.

After Barbara returned home and had said her good-nights to Robin and Diana, she found herself unable to sleep. She realized that she had felt understood by Alec in the way she felt understood by Judith and David. What was different, however, was that with Alec, on her side at least, the potential for combining friendship with passion was a reality.

Was there anything she wanted? he had asked. Had he been there with her at this moment she knew what she would have answered: she wanted Alec MacLeod. She wanted to experience again and again, not only the union that they shared as musicians, but the feeling of being seen and heard and understood, which had happened tonight. What their conversation had revealed to her was that here was a man with whom she could indeed have what Simon and Judith had found: passion *and* friendship. But did Alec find the same in her?

44

Although part of what had drawn him to Deborah was her pride in being a Jewish woman, David was relieved that they were being married from her home and not a synagogue. His great-grandfather had attended the synagogue of Bevis Marks regularly, his grandfather on high holy days, but he and his father only on rare occasions. It was hard enough for his father to accept his marriage to a penniless woman who would only hinder his social progress. He was glad that the ceremony, although religious, would be in somewhat neutral territory.

He was also relieved that Deborah's father had not forced on them the traditional full year's betrothal. He could not have waited that long, and he suspected that she was as eager as he to wed. Their embraces had become more and more passionate, and the closer they got to their wedding, the more eager David became.

He was grateful for his valet as he dressed that morning, for he found his hands were shaking in nervousness and anticipation. As his man smoothed the shoulders of his pearl-gray superfine and handed him his gloves and hat, he was almost paralyzed with fear, and it was only the memory of Deborah's candlelit face from that first Sabbath meal that energized him, and he was suddenly out the door before his man knew it.

The wedding was small, but even so, Mitre Street had eyes at every window as the Stanley carriage and the earl's coach pulled up. Robin lifted Diana down and was about to offer his hand to Barbara when he noticed Alec MacLeod at his side. So the wind lies that way, thought Robin, as he yielded to the other man and escorted his wife in.

Barbara, who had been adjusting her shawl, was expecting her brother, and the shock of surprise and pleasure at seeing Alec went right through her.

"May I escort you in, Lady Barbara?"

"Thank you, my lord," Barbara had time for only a quick glance around, but her eyes grew wide at the drabness of the neighborhood.

"Have you ever been to a Jewish wedding, my lord? I am not quite sure what to expect."

"I have not. I have heard, however, that it is a moving ceremony, followed by feasting and celebration."

And so it was. Perhaps because it was so different from the society weddings she had attended, Barbara found herself immeasurably moved when David walked into the room accompanied by his father and Mr. Cohen. Deborah was attended by Mrs. Treves and by Sarah.

Deborah stepped under the *chuppah,* the traditional canopy, where David was waiting and after the blessings and welcome, all turned to Sarah, waiting for the ring. She held out her hand, closed so tightly in a fist that her knuckles were white, and slowly opened her fingers, revealing the gold circle.

David placed the ring on Deborah's right hand, repeating after the rabbi: *"Haray aht m'kudeshet li b'tabba'at zu k'dat moshe v'yisrael."* ("Be you consecrated unto me by this ring in accordance with the laws of Moses and Israel.")

Barbara, who had smiled at the evidence of Sarah's concentration, felt tears welling up as the rabbi concluded his benediction. She was shaken out of her reverie, however, when David's foot smashed the glass, to remind everyone of the sorrow in life as well as the joy, and the Cohens' friends shouted *"Mazel tov!"*

Alec had disappeared from her side at some point, and when she heard the sound of the recessional, she realized why. The tune he was playing was unfamiliar to her and had a Spanish sound to it. Somehow, she felt he was playing it just for her, that he was speaking to her through his music, calling for her to celebrate love and life. Not just this particular love of David and Deborah, but all unions. It amazed her that Alec could move her that powerfully, and she had to remind herself that she was overly sensitive to music, after all.

But what music and celebration followed! Even Diana was shaken out of her reserve and joined the dancing, holding onto the corner of Robin's handkerchief and turning and turning with the music. Barbara danced with David and Mr. Cohen, but Alec was too busy playing to partner anyone. He played Ladino airs; he joined a neighborhood group of musicians for a few Polish tunes. And then he played a set of hornpipes and reels which had the guests improvising steps and whirling about in mock Highland flings.

It was, the exhausted Stanleys agreed, the most enjoyable wedding they had ever attended. Even Diana had to agree, as they rode slowly home, Robin sprawled out, his wife leaning against his arm, and Barbara on the seat opposite, her feet disgracefully resting on the carriage seat.

"Lord Alexander is responsible for this," grumbled Robin. "The man is inexhaustible. It is a pity there was no one there to match him, so we could have had him dancing his feet off."

Barbara felt herself blushing, and was grateful for the darkness of the carriage. Although he had not been near her, had never partnered her, she felt, irrationally, that she had been dancing with Alec all evening.

45

Alec himself was exhausted after the wedding. Even the well-worn calluses on his fingers had become sore from the constant playing. But he couldn't have helped himself. Something in the occasion, perhaps the wonderful juxtaposition of solemnity and celebration had called out to this mercurial nature, and it was as though he was being driven to play by something deep inside him. As Deborah's father had said in his toast, "*L'Chaim*." Alec had wanted to continue the toast, not just to life, but to love, to the newlyweds, and to the loveliest woman in the room, the love of his life, Barbara Stanley. Since he could hardly do that, he played every song for her, letting what he felt flow through and out of him, on the music. Of course, she could not have known, he thought, laughing at his own Celtic romanticism. But he didn't know if he had the patience to subject himself to a long wooing.

By the time he called on Barbara a few days after the wedding, however, he thought he had himself well in hand.

He was shown into the morning room, where Barbara and Diana were sipping tea.

"Come, my lord, and join us in a cup before we start our practice."

"Have you recovered from your playing?" Diana asked.

"Almost, although I do confess that my fingertips must now have calluses on their calluses. But it was a wild and wonderful wedding."

"Yes, I was just telling Barbara that it made me think

quite differently about Jewish people. I have never known any, really, except Sir David, and him only socially. I was very impressed by the ceremony."

"And Mr. Cohen was a wonderful dancer," teased Barbara. "He danced with Diana three times," she added in an aside to Alec.

"Disgraceful!"

"Actually," admitted Diana, "it was wonderful to be able to be carefree and not worry about what is done or not done. I very much enjoyed myself and Mr. Cohen is truly a wonderful dancer. Better than Robin."

"Diana, I am shocked!"

"Now, don't tease, Barbara, but it is often true that one's spouse is not always one's favorite dance partner. Sometimes with another man, one feels an instant rapport. On the dance floor, my dear. On the dance floor only," continued Diana repressively as Barbara started to laugh at the thought of the balding, stout Mr. Cohen and Lady Diana developing instant rapport. And yet they had, for everyone had commented upon the gracefulness of their dancing.

"We had better get busy, my lord," Barbara said to Alec. Perhaps we will be able to play the whole sonata today."

"Aye, that is what I had hoped."

"Well, don't be shy, you two," said Diana, letting them go.

As Alec watched Barbara walk down the hall in front of him, he could not help thinking that he and Barbara might always be each other's best partner, on and off the dance floor. The question was, how soon might he be able to convince her of this?

Barbara felt Alec's eyes on her and was quite unaccountably warm by the time she reached the music room. She sat down quickly at the piano. Instead of handing her the music, Alec leaned over her to place it in front of her.

This time, as Alec breathed near her cheek, Barbara turned toward him. His nose brushed hers, and their lips met lightly for a few seconds before Alec started to pull away.

"Don't stop," whispered Barbara, without thinking.

"Dinna fash yerself, lass," said Alec as he sat down beside her on the piano bench. "I am juist getting a wee bit more comfortable." Barbara opened her eyes and reached her hand up to touch his face.

"Oh, lassie," said Alec, falling even deeper into his Scottish lilt, "I dinna think I can wait any longer."

"For what?" she whispered.

"For this," he replied, and putting his arms around her, kissed her passionately and deeply.

As she began to respond, she waited for him to draw back, the way Wardour always had. Instead, as she hungrily nibbled at his lips, he only groaned and began to tease hers open.

"You are not going to stop?" she asked wonderingly.

"Stop? Not unless you want me to."

Instead of answering, Barbara drew his head down to hers and felt, paradoxically, that he was both satisfying every longing and, at the same time, making her want more, years more of him.

When at last they pulled away from each other, it was only to take a breath and be drawn like magnets into another embrace.

Alec pulled away first, and gave a long sigh.

Was he regretting it? thought Barbara. Did he think her shameless?

"You didn't enjoy that, my lord?" she asked, shocking herself by her boldness.

"Oh, lass, enjoy isna the word. It is only that I had not planned to do this."

"Well, neither had I, I assure you," she replied tartly. "We can forget it ever happened. I am no seventeen-year-old, you know."

"Thank God."

"Yes, I suppose you can be thankful," said Barbara, hurt

more than she had ever dreamed possible. "You don't have to worry that I will call 'compromise.'"

"Well, if you won't lass, then I will have to."

Alec stood up as though he were indeed going to open the music-room door and shout the word down the corridor.

"Alec," she said, grabbing his arm, "what had you not planned to do?"

"I had not planned to woo you like a bloody Celtic wild man, but in a dignified, slow Sassenach way. And I've blown it all to hell."

"Woo me?" asked Barbara.

"Yes, now that I can honestly, as myself. I could hardly have done it as Alec Gower. Especially with you betrothed to another man."

"I am almost twenty-seven, you know, quite on the shelf."

"And what would I want with a seventeen-year-old, I would like to know? I want you."

"Why?"

"All these questions, lass. Don't you believe me?"

"Oh, yes, I do," said Barbara softly. "But I wanted to help you to a more dignified wooing, my lord," she added with a twinkle in her eye.

"The reasons why I want you. This could take days, you know," said Alec.

"Then you had better get started, my lord."

Alec opened his mouth to speak and could not. It was as though all the reasons, all the loving words, had deserted him. He sat down on the bench again, close to Barbara, and opening his music to the andante, started to play the melody with his right hand. Quite naturally, Barbara lowered her head to his shoulder and let the music tell her everything he wished to say.

"I wrote it for you, you know," he whispered after the last note died away. "Were there reasons enough?"

"Oh, yes," she answered. "And a musician's wooing is more effective than a Scotsman's or a Sassenach's."

Epilogue

It was difficult for Barbara and Alec to get through the rest of the Season, which felt as if it would never end. They were bored by their social obligations and only wanted to spend time in each other's arms, which they did at every opportunity on the dance floor and on assorted balconies. They did not try to hide their joy, and their friends and acquaintances were delighted and eagerly awaited the wedding, which was to take place at Ashurst on Midsummer Day.

Some members of society, of course, thought it undignified for a woman of Lady Barbara Stanley's years to be floating around like an eighteen-year-old, especially after jilting someone like Wardour for a Scotsman, no matter that he was a duke's grandson. Barbara ignored them, and concentrated upon her own happiness.

This happiness was so great, and had come after such loneliness, that at times she could not believe in it and would worry that something dreadful would happen to prevent their marriage. She was in this state the night before the wedding, Midsummer's Eve, and was restlessly pacing around her bedroom when her glance fell on her prayer book, which was on the night table. She opened it, and there was the sprig of myrtle from last summer.

Should she? It had, after all, accurately predicted the course of the year. She had not married Wardour. No, she was being ridiculous. The myrtle would be there in the morning and then what would she feel? Disappointed? More anxious?

All of a sudden she remembered that morning with Alec in the clearing and the newly born feeling of joy that had filled her, and all her worry fell away. This was meant from the beginning, she thought, and whether the myrtle is there or not, nothing will change that. So here's to you, Madame Zenobia, and I will risk your charm again! And she slipped the book under her pillow.

In the morning she again became aware of the hard lump beneath her head and laughed at her late-night imaginings. She would not even open the book, for she knew what she would find. So she pulled on her dressing gown and rang for some chocolate. It was only after the maid had left that her curiosity got the better of her, and she opened the book.

The myrtle was gone. It had fallen out, she told herself. She looked under the pillow, under the sheets, under the bed. Nothing. The sprig of myrtle had disappeared as though it had been spirited away. And she most certainly was going to marry Alec MacLeod this morning and spend the rest of her life working to keep their joy in one another alive.

It was agreed that the small parish church had never held such a radiant bride. Or such a striking bridegroom. The women of Ashurst agreed that Lady Barbara had married herself a man with a fine pair of legs, and wasn't she a lucky one, for she would discover that night what was under a Scotsman's kilt, and wouldn't they make fine music together on their wedding night.

As indeed they did.